Karen

Marian Wells

BETHANY HOUSE PUBLISHERS
MINNEAPOLIS, MINNESOTA 55438
A Division of Bethany Fellowship, Inc.

Originally published under the title, *When Love Is Not Enough*

This edition, 1983

Scripture quotations are from the New English Bible
and the King James Version

Karen
Marian Wells

Library of Congress Catalog Card Number 83-71514

ISBN 0-87123-306-1

Published by Bethany House Publishers
A Division of Bethany Fellowship, Inc.
6820 Auto Club Road, Minneapolis, Minnesota 55438

Printed in the United States of America

The Author

MARIAN WELLS, born in Utah and educated at Northwestern Nazarene College, makes her home with her family in Arizona. A free-lance writer, she has written two books.

Chapter 1

The stairwell in the old mountain resort was built like a mine shaft: narrow, beamed, wood-lined, and full of dust motes dancing in the brilliance coming through the skylight. Bare wooden stairs wound steeply around the walls, falling into the darkness of the hall below.

A girl burst through the door at the top and clattered down the first flight. Then she paused even as her extended foot reached for the next step, listening, with her body straining forward. There was that sensation again. As her echoing footsteps died away, the oppressive quiet of the dark hall rose to meet her. Karen clutched her floating robe close and leaned over the railing. Why was she becoming increasingly aware of this sensation? In the quiet, alone times, why did she have this feeling of being not really alone? And why in unguarded moments like this did she find herself looking around expecting eyes that were never there?

Her mass of dark hair slid across her shoulder and, as she waited, she pulled the rough muslin of her dress more closely about her, making a cocoon of it. She wished it were. Wouldn't a cocoon guarantee that protection she needed? "A nice hard shell," she murmured, looking down at the muslin. "Oh, how I need one to protect me from this fearful day!"

The logical, confident Karen who should be in control tried to remind her other frightened self that the day wasn't fearful; it was only a dark tunnel towards true productivity. She grinned at her high flying thoughts and continued down the stairs.

As she stepped through the doorway into the lobby, on her left was a dark paneled wall holding an oversized poster of the divine master. Beneath the poster was a white-covered table, bearing twin candles and an arrangement of dried grasses.

Karen paused to study the bearded face and watchful eyes. Could the meditation that the master taught or could his portrait itself have anything to do with these strange feelings?

She could hear the wind stirring the tops of the pines that surrounded the mountain lodge. Across the room curtains billowed in the icy April air. The sun and the wind-lashed pines were working together to create flickering patterns of light and shadow that seemed to creep across the wall toward that poster.

Shivering in the sharp air, Karen went to close the windows. As the curtains collapsed against her hand, she looked at the poster. But as light and shadow had disappeared, the strange sensations had eluded her again.

Sighing with relief Karen walked briskly toward the fireplace. As she approached a cluster of rocking chairs near the fireplace, a man rose from one of them.

"There you are, Mark. I didn't see you scrunched down in that chair."

He seemed to mentally shake himself as he stood erect. Pointing to the canvas bag she carried, he said, "That means you're ready to go."

"Yes." She tried to make her voice decisive and wished she felt that way inside.

"The others want to ride into Denver with us. I'll see if they're ready."

Now she was free to say her farewells to the place she had called home for two years. She glanced around. The aging air of the lodge reminded Karen of a motherly housewife settling into middle age, content with her shabby dress and graying hair. With a rush of childlike insecurity, Karen realized how much she could miss the mother-love of the place.

A shadow in the corner moved and Karen saw the other occupant of the room. "Lenny, I didn't know you were here, too."

"I was meditating." His voice was gentle and slow. "Have you had yours?"

"I'm going to miss meditating in such serene surroundings."

"It doesn't matter where you do it; just don't forget." The expression in his pale blue eyes became concerned. "The world you are moving back into is a hostile one."

He tented his fingers together under his chin. "We believe it necessary to spread the art of meditating, but don't expect it to be easily accepted." Now he smiled down at her. "Not all are as eager and accepting as you."

"Lenny," she chided softly, "after two years of learning and meditating, I'm completely convinced this is all very necessary; but I'm not that gullible. Besides, you've forgotten, I know Denver. I lived and worked there for two years."

"And now you're going back." Coming from the hallway, the voice conveyed disappointment. Karen turned. Bella, she saw, was wearing that horrible pants suit again. Besides last week's rip, now a button was missing from the jacket.

Bella fumbled with the gaping jacket as she continued her conversation. "Karen, this bothers me terribly. Since you've made this decision, you haven't had a minute's peace. You've crept around this place like you've seen a ghost. That doesn't seem like a valid way to live out your mission in life."

Karen tried to smile. "Peace and love? Are they always easy? Since I first came, you and Lenny have been hammering it into me that I'm obligated to spread this message to others. I've wondered how it could be managed, especially here. I need a few pupils. I don't think the deer and chipmunks are candidates, at least not in their present unevolved state."

"You needn't make a joke of it all," Lenny said. "Bella is serious. I've noticed, too, that you're almost as overwrought as you were when you first arrived here."

Karen closed her eyes. "Oh, please, Lenny, that isn't possible! I am serious. I've really racked my brain for a way to do what I'm supposed to be doing and in a way that I feel I can cope with. Do you believe in destiny? Why did I just happen to turn on the radio that day and just happen to hear about that auto accident? Why do I feel as if I'm being pushed out the door, forced back into life in exactly the same place I exited?"

Her voice dropped and she couldn't keep the tremor out of it. "Oh, Lenny, I don't want it that way. I'm being crushed by all that I've learned. And if I believe those things, I dare not disobey. If it is really within my power to change the force of evil in his life, to break the chain of wrong doing when I was the one to create those ugly links in the first place, well, then, I've no choice. There, end of speech."

They clustered around her, and more words burst out. "But, I'm so scared. I've never pushed my ideas on anyone before. I know it's important. This wonderful feeling is something I've unconsciously searched for all my life, and I think this way of being in tune with the universe is something I'm obligated to talk about." Lisa pressed close for a moment and Bella came to put her own blue crocheted shawl in Karen's arms as Mark reached for the canvas bag.

As they all started for the door, Karen determined she would not look back. But as she left the room her footsteps echoed, reminding her that behind her the room was empty now.

As the van scooted toward the curb in front of the Denver Dry Goods store, Karen rocked in her seat. She saw the spot was marked "No Parking," and immediately outraged vehicles blasted their disapproval.

Rubbing the tense muscles in her neck, she tried not to think about trees and mountains, peace and quiet. Beside her Lisa had her nose against the window in that eager, little-girl way. "Oh, Karen, how could you come back to this? They aren't even real. Look at the women. Their faces are all painted into the same expressions and the men—" Words failed her and she turned to Karen. "We had it so good up there. This place hurt you terribly. Why must you come back?"

Karen put her fingers against Lisa's lips to stop the tumbling, accusing words. Then she wrapped her arms around the younger girl and pressed her face against Lisa's. "There, Little Rosebud, don't fret. You're too young to understand all these things." She smiled down at Lisa and, in an attempt to keep the emotion out of her voice, drawled, "Just trust old Karen to finally figure out what's right and do it. This isn't the end of the world. I'll be back to see you." Quickly she kissed Lisa and slid back across the seat.

"You okay, Karen? Sure you don't want to change your mind?" Lenny was leaning over the seat. He held her old canvas bag as if he really didn't intend to turn it loose. She nodded and tugged at the bag.

Now Bella leaned forward to pull the blue crocheted shawl closer around Karen. She was only twenty-six, two years older than Karen, but she had mothered everyone at the commune. "Lenny," her dark eyes were taking in every detail of Karen's expression and dress, "leave her alone.

You know that what she's doing has its basis in the master's writings. What must be, must be. We are all called to be healers of the spirit. If she feels this is the right way, let her do it."

Karen glanced briefly out the window at the surge of humanity passing on the street and then looked around at the occupants of the van. "You dear people." She touched Bella's cheek. "Compared to that out there, you are all a bunch of fresh meadow flowers, all untainted and individual. My beautiful garden and how I hate to leave it!"

Their voices rose in a chorus. Their advice was falling like the flower petals she had imagined and her lips curled with amusement at the picture of them straining against their roots, nodding in the breeze. In a hidden corner of her thoughts, she realized she was easing past the difficult moment that she had been dreading for almost a month.

"Karen, you can always come back."

"Remember, we love you."

"Sow peace and serenity and don't forget: meditate twenty minutes twice a day. You'll ruin it all if you forget."

Mark had merely listened to all of the conversation to this point. But now he admonished, "Forget the past and all of the hurt. That's bad karma. Forgetting is the only way. You can't continue on the gross level. And what you must do, do without thinking of that past. It could destroy you. Think only of the endless future." His serious eyes floated away in the dimness and he went back to the wheel.

Again Lenny was protesting, "Karen, you know this isn't necessary."

"Yes, it is necessary." Her voice was low and patient. He leaned over the back of her seat and pushed aside the dark mop of hair until he could see her eyes. "See," she insisted, "even Mark recognizes the necessity of it all."

Lenny's expression was very serious as he studied her face. She knew that was because he had been there since the beginning. He and Bella. They had been with her during the worst times. Sometimes she thought they didn't yet believe the bad times were over.

Lisa had her nose to the window again. "Look at those people in their ridiculous clothes, posing as if their fine rags made them real people." Her voice was scornful. "They're only sticks supporting those fashion plate clothes. Look, they wear them like a uniform. The leather and turtle necks are the leisure uniforms. The business suits and brief cases are the uniforms of the successful."

She turned to Karen. "Oh, sorry. For a moment I'd forgotten you were into the fashion business. I'm so used to seeing you like this, I'd quit thinking."

Bella's face puckered into a worried frown. "Karen, you needn't dress like last year's street people. There's nothing about meditating that indicates you have to look different. The differences must be on the inside."

"But she's had to go the whole route of changing her life," Lenny said. "She'll get over the sore thumb image soon enough."

"It isn't that," Karen explained. "It's just that I've dressed this way for so long. Now it's too much of a shock to think of establishment clothes on top of having to return to Denver."

The horns renewed their blast. "Sure you don't want us to drop you off at the hospital?" Mark asked from his seat behind the wheel.

"No." Karen rose reluctantly and made her way to the door. Her bag was handed down and the van puffed off without further good-byes. She was grateful for that.

She stood on the curb and slowly turned. From her position she studied everything on the street. It was achingly familiar, yet strange. Two years of mountains and quiet somehow made the street seem alien.

With the first break in the pack of people, Karen scooted across the sidewalk to stand in front of The Denver's display windows. It was shocking to see how much fashions had changed during the past two years. Even as she studied the display, she felt the familiar curious urge to create. That skirt line was wrong. She knew she could improve on the bulkiness of that jacket.

At first, as she studied the windows, she saw only the strange new mannequins with their iron-curled hair and hooded eyes, postured in haughty coolness. Now she became aware of the men. They were a hidden row behind the women. She could see they were meant to be a statement of women's rights. They were only a background, with no more importance than a vase of flowers or a draped table. It was the exalted female in center stage. The scene seemed all wrong to her and, without understanding why, she felt her lips curl with scorn.

One of the male mannequins was a tall, lean redhead. He made her think of Irish. What had two years done to Mr. Daniel St Clair? Was he the stereotype modern male, a figurehead in a female world? She laughed aloud at the idea. That arrogant man wrapped in his studied success image content to be a backdrop?

Her laughter ended in a sigh and she turned away from the window. An edge of her carefully won peace was crumbling into misery. It was the old familiar misery.

As Karen stepped into the stream of people, a woman carrying a baby approached. The infant was squalling. She could see the tiny red face beneath the knitted cap was suffused with agony. Miniature balled fists thrashed the air. As they passed Karen, one frantic, damp hand grazed her cheek. With a surprised gasp she spun across the sidewalk.

The woman stopped. "Oh, dear, did we hurt you?" The baby thrashed and squalled louder.

Karen concentrated on the compassion in the mother's eyes. "No, oh, no." She could hardly speak above the unexpected pounding of her heart. "I was only startled." She forced a strained smile and ducked away from the bobbing red face.

Karen's hands were trembling as she tried to hold the shawl around her shoulders. She was bitterly regretting her decision to ride the bus to the hospital. Downtown Denver was just too much all at once.

To quiet the churning emotion, she tried to think about the friends she had left. "Mark said I had to forget," she murmured. "The past is gone. It will never be again and it must be forgotten."

At the lodge they had told her past mistakes were on the gross level of living and she must forget them, because her life was no longer to be lived on that level. For a fraction of a moment she was haunted by the spector of future mistakes. She squeezed her eyes shut. "Oh, no!"

She crashed into a soft, warm obstacle. "Oh, sorry, are you okay?" Karen asked the grandmotherly lady. Seeing the nod, she hurried on.

The bus that would take her to the hospital was approaching and she turned to cross the street. Her long muslin dress twisted around her ankles and the leather sandals flapped against her heels as she hurried. Mountain garb wasn't suited for city streets. But then, Karen admitted sadly as she dropped her money into the driver's hand, neither am I.

Two years is a long time and she acknowledged the fact that she could never fit into the old niches again. *But you needn't*, she reminded herself. *Only do your duty and then go.*

For the rest of the ride, her thoughts were full of a silent, serene, always-smiling Karen, floating about creating a mood of peace everywhere she went. She wondered if she could hang onto that image.

The bus bounced across the winter-pocked asphalt to the corner. It creaked to a stop and Karen could only sit staring at the hospital. "Okay, kid," the driver pivoted to look at her. "Here's your hospital."

Curious faces turned toward her. Karen gathered her

bag and shawl and left the bus. The doors clanged shut and when the cloud of dust settled, she was left facing the cold granite building across the street. Its trees and bushes, even the flowers and postage-stamp park on Karen's side of the street, failed to detract from the forbidding air.

Karen backed up and sat down on the bench under the bus stop sign. Beside the bench, in the corner of the park, a shrub-edged circle was vivid with yellow and flame tulips.

She eyed them and wondered if she should have brought flowers. But then flowers and Irish didn't seem to go together.

Now Karen noticed the woman sitting on the other end of the bench. She was studying Karen with squirrel-quick glances. Karen swallowed a chuckle as she acknowledged the woman's resemblance to the friendly Denver squirrels. Her cinnamon brown suit topped with a soft gray fur was the perfect touch to the picture. Karen smiled and the woman smiled back.

Scooting around, Karen looked at the building again and wondered where she would find the courage to cross that street and ask the questions she must ask. She must remember to say "Daniel," not "Irish."

The memory of Irish was something she had been constantly squelching for the past two years. In fact, she admitted, she had avoided the memory as if her life depended on forgetting. Now that memory must be faced. Would her new-found strengths and beliefs see her through this difficult time?

She tried to shape her lips over the name, Daniel St Clair.

Karen glanced towards the other end of the bench and met the woman's eyes. She addressed the curious eyes, the gray waves of hair and the kid gloves. "My husband is in that hospital."

Instantly the woman's expression became maternal and interested, "And you've come to see him. Is he ill?"

"No, it was a horrible automobile accident. In Wyoming with a semi."

"Then he's a truck driver?"

Karen shook her head. "No. I don't know what he was doing in Wyoming." She was aware of the woman's scrutiny, the raised eyebrows. It was obvious she was taking in all the details of Karen's dress—the muslin that dragged in the dust, the flimsy shawl, and the sandals. Even her hair didn't escape that knowing look, and Karen was ashamed of its scraggly untidiness and wished it were a neat, silky fall like Lisa's.

From the growing look of scorn, Karen knew she was in too deep to escape now. She hugged the bulging canvas bag and continued. "He's been there over a month and I've been trying all this time to get up enough nerve to go see him."

The woman looked shocked and Karen felt her faulty composure failing. She licked her dry lips. "We haven't lived together for ages. Almost two years ago I joined a commune up above Ward."

Until that moment the commune had been a wonderful place. Karen watched the distaste almost crowd out the curiosity on the woman's face.

Reluctantly she said, "It's a religious-type thing. The reason I've come back now is that I see how selfish it is to live up there and keep all that peace and serenity to myself. No—" she was silent a moment, "that isn't quite honest and I must be." She pressed her fingers against her eyes for a moment.

"There's so much life that has to be changed before you can really make progress. I was getting to the place where I needed to do something about all the bad karma." She threw a quick glance at the woman. "It's necessary if you want to meditate successfully."

The bewildered expression on the woman's face grew. Did she move farther away? At the commune everyone talked the same language. They even thought alike. There, peace and serenity were a way of life. Now here, away from the commune, Karen felt helplessly adrift. How could she learn to communicate in a world she had forgotten?

She realized she would have to be the one to bridge the gap. Without knowledge there could be no understanding. Now would be a good time to start. Unquestionably, this woman would be easier to handle than Irish.

"In order to be a complete person," Karen explained, "that is, to experience real oneness, I've had to come back. There was so much in the past that was interrupting. The bad karma was influencing me until the vibes were all wrong and I wasn't getting any place with my meditation."

The woman's carefully arranged smile was slipping around the edges and Karen tried to explain. "This whole business, even the accident, is all my fault. Do you understand? My karma, . . . you know . . . all the forces created by my evil actions, were hurting him. All the bad vibrations surrounding him were really caused by me, by my bad living. Don't you see? It's terrible to understand your responsibility and not do something about it. You know, I've realized all this for a long time, but, until the accident, I thought somehow I could avoid facing it. No matter how badly I hated to leave that wonderful place and come back to all this terrible karma I've created, I just had to. And I've got to do it all quickly before something else happens."

Karen had forgotten the woman's presence. Lost in thought she whispered, "If I don't face this now, who knows what someone will suffer because of me? Perhaps even generations and generations from now I could be responsible for some terrible tragedy."

"Child," the woman said sharply. Startled back to reality, Karen looked at her. "You're being too emotional." She reached a gloved hand to Karen. "I'm sure you must have had a reason to leave him in the first place. An automobile accident? He doesn't sound too dependable to me."

"Oh, no, you've got it all wrong." Karen looked down at the muslin dress and realized the mental picture she had created. "Irish isn't like that at all. He's so establishment he could pass for your son." Karen paused, not sure she should have described him quite like that. "On top of that he's an attorney." She couldn't keep the bitter note out of her voice. "He's 'one of Denver's most promising young men'—I'm quoting."

Karen found herself trying to rub out the unhappy picture she had created. As she talked she discovered she was caught up in a wistful yearning she hadn't allowed during the past two years.

"Irish is so handsome it makes your heart hurt. He's the kind of guy you're not afraid to trust. But he really just looks too good to be true. He's tall and thin. Too thin. It makes his shoulders look terribly wide. He's got red hair and eyes that are gray until he gets angry; then they're green."

She stopped, confused. The woman was smiling gently and Karen wondered why. "And you love him. You're just like the rest of us foolish women with stars in our eyes. To you he's assumed all the proportions of a god, and he can kick you around and you'll still love him." The woman's voice grated and momentarily her gentle mask slipped. Karen got a peek at the pain this woman had endured.

Karen was shaking her head, slowly but insistently. She could see the woman's smile was bitter, hurt, and she wanted to reach out to erase the hurt, but she could only ache inside as the woman got up to board her bus. Karen watched her leave, still wearing the bitter smile.

The wind tumbled Karen's hair and tangled her skirt around her ankles. With a tired sigh she pushed the hair out of her eyes. *Are women always born to be losers? That would make a good riddle*, she thought wryly. *When is winning losing? When you get married, of course*, was her reply.

The bus disappeared from sight and Karen sat down again, still filled with the burden of the things she didn't say. But could she have put them into words? It was hard even to think about them. How about explaining the way Irish's haughty arrogance could give way to tenderness and how the gray eyes sometimes, in unguarded moments, looked at the world as if he were again that uncertain, shabby little boy watching life from the outside.

She needed to sternly remind herself that in the end he hadn't been that way at all. Tenderness changes and becomes steel when a man must fight and scratch to realize his goals.

It had been frightening, she allowed herself to remember, to see the tenderness go, to see him become cold, even calculating. The end began when the coldness was turned on her.

She straightened and looked across the street. The hospital was gray granite. Its April afternoon shadows were deeper gray. Gray was a cool and aloof color. She shivered in the spring's pale sunlight and pulled the shawl tight. Slowly she got to her feet and slowly she started toward the gray building.

Chapter 2

Irish opened his eyes. The view today was blue sky. He knew it was pain that had interrupted his way through the haze they called sleep, and he knew it was soon time for another pain pill.

A white cap and blonde curls moved into view.

Daniel St Clair moistened his lips and said, "Come closer, Nurse. I can't read your name tag." She obliged. "Miss Christina Christopherson, R.N. Hi, Miss Tina."

"As often as you've read that in the past three weeks, you should be able to see it clear across the room." Now she was smiling down at him, smoothing and straightening the sheets, futilely attempting to make him more comfortable.

Wistfully he studied every line of her face. She would think him a perfect idiot if she knew the thoughts buzzing around in his head. She was his oasis. He was a bobbing balloon, buffeted by the capricious wind of pain. She held his string. He was deadwood, but under her hand, through her smile, he was learning to live again. And that was a miracle; not only to live again, but even to come to know his life had been so barren.

He took a deep breath and continued the conversation that had been running on the installment plan for the past two weeks. "This is all like a string of pearls, gray ones. Does that sound romantic? It isn't. After years of taking each bright clear day for granted—me bright and clear, not the day—I suddenly get served up with a whole string of these gray blobs. I guess I shouldn't complain. At least I know they're blobs now, not just a long, gray tunnel."

"Daniel St Clair, stop your fussing. It won't last forever." There was the faintest lilt of a Swedish accent in her voice.

He smiled up at her. "How's the world out there? Trees budding yet?"

"If you're interested enough to ask, then you'll make it. They're starting to show a good green. Anything else you'd like to know?"

"Yes, how about a date tonight? Dinner at Cherry Hills Club and a concert?"

"I'm ready. Are you?" She turned briskly and the door closed after her.

"Period." Irish muttered. "Conversation to be resumed when it's turning time." He reviewed his inane conversation and was oppressed by the burden of the things he wanted to say.

He remembered hearing that starving people often don't realize they are starving until appetite has been stimulated again. "I guess these are hunger pangs," he muttered as he fumbled for the book on the table beside him.

"Time for turning." Her voice was extra gentle and he knew it was because she was the type to sympathize. He gritted his teeth and waited for the pain.

She stood beside the table, fingering the books shoved in between the kidney-shaped basin and the jug of water. When he could breathe comfortably again, she asked, "You're interested in law?"

"I am an attorney."

"Were you doing fascinating things before the accident?"

"Not so much fascinating," he said slowly, "as sticky. What's the date?"

"March 28."

"Well, I should be in the middle of a decision today. The accident made that unnecessary. Maybe it's—what's the saying? A blessing in disguise."

She filled the glass with fresh water and held the straw to his lips. His hand curved around hers and he sensed the tension in her body. "Tina, come closer. You smell like April violets in the rain. You're better for me than fresh air and sunshine."

"Dan, you suffer from hospital fever. When you men are flat on your back, nurses always look like angels." He tugged at her hand. The effort shot pain along his back and leg and he gasped.

She was there immediately, and, as he waited for the pain to ease, he slipped his hand around her waist. "It's an excuse," she accused. He managed to grin. Bending over she tugged gently at the three weeks' growth of beard. "Behave yourself. Just because that red beard makes you look like a Viking, you needn't act like one."

The footsteps in the hall stopped. "Well, Danny boy, I see you're up to your old tricks." It wasn't a hospital-quiet voice and Irish winced as he recognized it. Releasing Tina, he looked beyond her to the men standing in the doorway.

"Well, Markham," he attempted to make his voice jovial. After all, it was Markham's money that was keeping him going now. "Didn't expect you to take time to come up here."

"I've been checking in often, Danny boy. You just haven't spent too much time talking." The words only hit the surface of Irish's mind. He was busy analyzing the man who had engaged his services. While the man's oily charm swept the conversation along, Irish became aware of one more reason Markham's proposition filled him with uneasiness. It was his eyes. That cold, remote expression didn't tally with the buddy-boy friendliness.

He noticed that while Markham talked he was appraising Tina. Irish was only mildly amused and Tina's manner contained more than a hint of her usual professional starch as she left the room.

Now Markham introduced his companion. As Irish studied the brown, pin-striped suit and the innocuous briefcase, he decided Markham's oiliness was a good counterbalance for the hot-house warmth this man exuded.

This Pete Norris was from the petroleum company Markham represented. As Irish listened to the conversational ball bounce slickly between the two of them, his uneasiness grew.

"Look, Mr. Norris," he interrupted.

The broad protesting palm. "Pete, if you please."

"Pete, there isn't much I can do from this position. It looks like I might spend as much as another three weeks here. The doc says the disc operation was successful, but the damaged nerves will probably affect my left leg. He's talked about therapy in another week if I continue this progress. Right now I realize it will be some time before I can make it on my own. You know I batch it and that kind of life'll slow me down for a while."

"Look," Markham interjected, "you didn't read me right. Certainly we need you back in there plugging as soon as possible. I'll level with you. Bloomington has the impression you'll be the guy taking over his spread, and he's being pretty stubborn about talking to anyone else. We want that land. That makes you pretty important to us."

"Wait a minute," Irish protested. "That wasn't part of the deal. I've only agreed to help you buy that land for long-term investment purposes."

"Right, St Clair," Markham said hastily. "We played you fair and square on that. You know, I'd have done at least part of the leg work myself, but I just don't have the time—plus the legal savvy to handle it. There's no sense complicating the whole deal with my bumbling."

Irish watched the man as he talked. Again he was troubled by a nagging sense of uneasiness. A hunch, he'd always labeled it. But in the past, hunches had been good things to investigate. Deliberately he closed his mind to the nagging feeling, even as he admitted to himself that it didn't seem to be a thing a smart attorney would do.

"Back to Bloomington. He's fallen for that farm boy look. What did you say that gave him the idea you'd consider chucking the lawyer business for herding cows?"

"I didn't say anything. I'd only admired his herd and envied the peace and quiet."

"Well, if he wants you, he'll get you even if we have to turn you into a gentleman farmer. What's attorney fees for herding cattle for say a year?" He chuckled and rubbed his hands together. "Come to think of it, it could be pretty nice to recuperate there, especially with that cute little nurse."

"Tina?"

"You just said you'd need help. We're prepared to finance you until you're back on your feet. I guess we owe you that much, since you were on a business trip for us when it happened," Pete said. He hastily added, "Now that's off the record. We'd deny the whole thing. But off the record, you're our key to the deal. Old man Bloomington has taken a shine to you, it's easy to see, and he has complete confidence in what you're doing. The sooner you're out of this hospital—even if it costs us for a private nurse and a physical therapist—the more valuable you are to us." He extended his hand and rubbed his fingers together.

His grin answered Irish's questions. Money. That big fat fee would be bigger. But Tina—that was even more exciting. He took a deep breath and tried to organize his thoughts.

The two men left and he was alone. After the accident and surgery, when he had first become aware of his surroundings, Tina had been there. Any male in any situation would have found it easy to fall in love with her, but that didn't explain why a nurse like Tina would show every indication of falling in love with a patient.

Irish tucked his hands under his head and stared at the ceiling. "Well, Markham, old buddy," he drawled, "you might just have a deal. This is sounding better all the time."

When Tina came again he was facing the window. The graying sky was filled with pink and yellow washed clouds. "How soon does a guy in my condition get out of here?"

"Don't you like the service?"

"Come around here and say that, closer." She waved the needle at his groping hand. "No, seriously."

"If it were just a common old disc, you'd be out walking the halls now. With you, I don't know." He heard the syringe clatter on the table top and her uniform rustled as she came around the bed. "Why?"

He looked at her serious blue eyes and felt his throat tighten. It had been a long time since anyone had looked at him like that. "You have the softest jaw line. I can't believe there's bone in there. Come here and let me check."

Her full lips curved upward. "You'd better believe it. I didn't get to be head nurse with boneless mush in there."

"Would you mind giving it up?" He grinned up at her surprised blushes and said, "Those fellows are my clients and they're pretty anxious for me to join the mainstream of life again. They've even indicated they'll support a private nurse. I just thought you'd fill the bill."

"I'm due a month's vacation and haven't made any plans," she said deliberately. "But aren't they pushing things? Surely some other lawyer could handle their affairs. You need time to recuperate."

"That's what I suggested, but this is a land deal involving an old man with a bad case of arthritis and a passionate attachment to his home acres."

"Somehow," she mused, "I get the feeling you aren't properly enthused about the whole affair."

"I'm not," he said slowly. "I can't explain it now. It's one of those situations that hold enough shadows to make you want to give it a long second look. It'll be good for my career if I pull the right strings at the right time. Right now I'm worried about hidden strings. The final deal isn't shady. It's just the method of getting there."

"Dan," her face was troubled, "I'm off in ten minutes. Let me go finish my charts and then I'll come back and listen."

She was gone before he could answer. Furious at himself, he listened to the door whisper shut and wondered how he had stepped into this hole.

"Look," he said when she stepped through the door again. "I'm a lawyer. I don't go around talking about my client's affairs."

"And I'm a nurse. I work under the same rule of confidentiality. I'd had the impression you needed to get it off your chest." Her cheeks were red and her eyes sparkled with indignation. "If you want to talk, fine. Otherwise I'll leave."

"When you sizzle like that, I'd talk about the man in the moon. Tina, come closer, I may need to whisper." He chuckled as she snorted and reached for her handbag and coat.

"Okay, you win." He watched her drop her things on the chair and circle the bed. Abruptly he was filled with an aching need for her. Her sensible maturity was as appealing as her physical charms, and most certainly she could supply that missing link in his life.

"Do you suppose," he asked slowly, "that marriage was invented because it takes two minds and combined strengths to make a success of life?"

For a moment she held her breath as if she were seriously considering the question. After a pause she said, "No, there are too many contented singles to make that theory absolutely correct."

"Are you a contented single?"

"Dan, I'm here to listen to you."

He tried to give his attention to his story, to sort the facts and present them in a way that would help Tina understand the situation. He found his thoughts were full of the picture of her always there, not constantly flying out the door, leaving him frustrated and dangling in mid-sentence.

He moved restlessly and brought his attention back to the story. "If I were to mention the name of the oil company Markham is representing, you'd recognize it as one of the more successful, so we'll just forget names for now. A little over six weeks ago, Mr. Markham came to my office and plopped down a big, fat retainer fee. It seems there's a ranch in Wyoming they want me to purchase in the interests of their company. That is, with their money to back it, but set up under a different corporate name."

Tina had a perplexed frown on her face and Irish could guess her thoughts. "Do you understand, Tina? I'm at the stage in my career where I spend more time polishing office furniture than I do taking important clients to lunch."

"You think it's too good to be true?"

"I think it sounds as if I may have to wear blinders while I handle the affair. But the situation certainly isn't unheard of. It is possible to be ethical without placing all of your cards on the table."

"Do you," she asked slowly, "have an associate or someone higher up referring people like Mr. Markham to you?"

"No, no rich uncle lawyer. This fact is making me a trifle uneasy. Want to hear more?"

She nodded and he continued, "Markham laid his cards straight. There'll be no room for misunderstanding in this deal, which I appreciate. As far as I can see the total picture, he's playing it fair with me and I'd say this is only a smart move by a shrewd businessman." He paused briefly and then carefully said, "If you want to be realistic, it is something an ambitious businessman who operates in the gray areas of morality would be expected to pursue."

"Why is it bothering you?" Tina asked slowly. "Are you afraid of your reputation being hurt?"

"Of course. I can't afford to make a mistake." She seemed disappointed. "He was emphatic in stressing that his name, as well as the oil company's name, be kept out of the picture at this time." Irish continued, "He explained it like this: Right now they have no way of knowing whether or not there's oil on the land. According to Markham, the only attractive features about the place are the price and the fact the acreage extends right up to the edge of oil-producing land. Another large company owns this adjoining land."

"Why hasn't the other company purchased this ranch?"

"Because the ranch's owner, Mr. Bloomington, isn't working out in the open. There were only a few who knew it was on the market. How Markham got wind of it, I don't know."

"It seems strange your Mr. Bloomington would sell that way."

"He feels the future of the ranch is more important than money. He's kind of a fuddy-duddy old man who thinks this energy crisis is going to blow over before anyone will seriously consider digging for oil on his land. While Markham has insisted they want this purely for speculation, he says they will continue to run the ranch for a number of years. This is precisely what Bloomington wants. Markham has assured me that the only reason they want their name kept out of the deal is because he thinks Bloomington is going to jump to conclusions if he hears the word oil. I'm inclined to agree with him. Also, it doesn't take much to figure out the types of clauses Bloomington will stick on the deal if oil is mentioned. I'm positive Markham won't even consider the deal if he can't get the mineral rights at the same time."

Thoughtfully she said, "He could be a completely forthright man just looking for the easiest way to acquire land."

"Could be. Markham has indicated they'll hang on to the acreage until the market runs the price up. Then they'll sell."

"Why won't they develop the land themselves?"

"According to him they have all they can handle for the next thirty years. It's just that with all this talk about alternative energy, any investment in Wyoming looks good."

"Dan, all this leaves me feeling like I'm on a merry-go-round. I keep getting a glimpse of something, but it's out of sight before I can understand it."

"Wait, you haven't heard it all. There's a rumor," he paused and chewed at his lip. "I guess I should have investigated it before now. Anyway, the grapevine indicates Markham's company is having real financial problems."

The silence became painful before Tina spoke again. "Why don't you just ship the retainer fee back to them and ask them to find another lawyer?"

Irish knew he looked as embarrassed as he felt. "I pulled a dumb stunt. I was so confident it was a sure thing that before I went to Wyoming, I moved into a new condominium complex and bought some furniture. I never guessed I'd come back from Wyoming with a great big question mark hanging over the whole deal, or," he felt his lips twist into a wry grin, "or that I'd come home flat on my back." Tina looked shocked and troubled. Obviously there was something she wanted to say, and he waited. After a moment of silence she stepped closer to the bed and Irish went on. "With the bank check in my pocket and the preliminary papers ready to be signed, I didn't have any qualms at all. I intended to see the ranch and exclaim over a few cows, deliver the check and get back home. It wasn't that simple. Mr. Bloomington is in his seventies and is quite crippled with arthritis. I ended up feeling all sorry and obligated to the poor guy."

Irish lay staring out the window. He was wondering how

he could express the emotional upheaval his trip to Wyoming had generated.

"Tina, I was born and raised in New York. Surroundings have always been impersonal things to me. The landscape was a patch of grass dotted with very few flowers and trees, and circled by sidewalks and tall gray buildings. In the four years I've lived in Denver, this is the first time I've driven to Wyoming and the first time I've been forced to really look at my surroundings.

"Wyoming is overwhelming. It isn't a matter of beauty but instead of powerful immensity. It's just there, take it or leave it. It makes you feel as if life has been stripped down to essentials, and I guess it has. The gray hills and sagebrush, the clear air and uninterrupted sun leave you feeling like a blot on the landscape. First thing I did was take off my tie and hide it in my pocket."

Tina chuckled and he continued, "The evening I arrived, I was treated to a complete history of the land—that is after Mrs. Bloomington finished stuffing me with the best beef I've ever eaten. I don't know how people can eat like that and stay as thin as weather-beaten fence posts."

Irish gingerly shifted his position and went on with the story. "The Bloomington land has been in the family since great grandfather Bloomington homesteaded the land over a hundred years ago. His first neighbors were Indians and, to prove they weren't always friendly, Mr. Bloomington took me out to see the evidence. There's a fort out behind the present family home. It's constructed of logs thicker than a man's body. Mr. Bloomington pointed out the arrow heads still sticking in those logs and all uncomfortably close to the gun slots."

"Sounds interesting. I'd love to see it."

He remembered Markham's proposal and wondered how Tina would fit in that barren land. "The farmhouse is comfortable," he said slowly. "It's a two-story with an old-fashioned veranda on three sides of it. Mrs. Bloomington has a patch of grass in the front yard with a few trees and flowers."

He shifted his position and looked at Tina. "After two days of driving a jeep over the property and exclaiming over cows, I was left with a completely different picture of the whole affair. I don't have any doubts. Mr. Bloomington intends his ranch to continue in the same tradition—cows and alfalfa. Markham is going to be hard pressed to get that land without a string of clauses attached, and I'm the one who's going to have to bring this whole situation together. Right now that sounds pretty impossible. While I was there I didn't offer the check. It was easy to see they were still trying to talk themselves into selling."

"If they love it so, why are they leaving?"

"Mr. Bloomington says he needs a warmer climate for his health." Now Irish was thinking aloud. "That land is fascinating. It rolls on forever, not making promises, just being Wyoming. If I hadn't seen it through their eyes and felt their pride in it, I don't believe I'd put much of a value on it. They treated that land like a living entity. Obviously they don't want to leave. The more they talked, the more it came through. That harsh country has made a broken old man out of Bloomington, but still he loves it all."

"And you're obligated to buy it for Markham."

"There's always a chance, and a very big one, that there isn't any oil up there." They stared at each other and Tina sighed with relief.

"Dan, you don't really think there's oil, do you?" she asked. He grinned and hoped his grin was more confident than he felt.

The next day Irish was out of bed. With Tina on one side and the doctor on the other, he made his first tentative steps since the accident that had crushed a disc in his spine. Perspiration rolled down his cheeks and into his beard and his left leg dragged.

"As soon as you master the locomotion and can get in and out of bed without help," the doctor said, "then I'll dismiss you with the provision you have nursing care and therapy. You'll probably be having trouble with muscle cramps and will need medication for pain."

"I am now," he rubbed at the perspiration. "Does inactivity have anything to do with it?" The doctor nodded and reached for a prescription pad.

Chapter 3

It was during visiting hours three days later that Irish's door swung open and Tina came into the room. From the bed he watched her lean against the door as if she were trying to hold it closed. Her eyes were deeply shadowed today and he noticed that she seemed pale. "Do you," she asked slowly, "Dan, do you know someone who calls you 'Irish'?"

He dropped the magazine he held and felt his face twist with pain. "Tina, I think I'm going to need that medication now."

When she came back into the room her face was rigid. She asked, "Dan, are you married?"

How could he have thought the past could be forgotten? "Tina, I should have—" he stopped. He could apologize, but that was presuming an intimacy that had never really been there.

Her hands trembled as she sponged his arm. She had asked and she had reacted. With a sensation of turning a page he would rather not turn, he asked, "How did you know?"

"There's a woman at the desk. She called you Irish and said she was your wife."

Tina plunged the needle into his arm and the pain was a

catalyst to his bitter thoughts. She put the syringe on the table and bent over him. "Tina, I don't want to remember. Let's not talk about it." She was shaking her head slowly and insistently, and he knew Karen was suddenly between them and would remain there until he did something about it.

When she finally spoke, her words were thoughtful. "You've been deeply hurt, haven't you?"

He was grateful for the understanding and found he could begin to explain. "Karen's been gone two years. Without a word, she just walked out. I'd thought we had a pretty good marriage. After the initial hurt and disappointment, I've had two years of relative peace and I want it to stay that way. Does that tell you anything about us?"

"What is she like? Where did you meet her?"

"I'd just finished law school and had passed my bar exams, and I was on my way back to Denver to open a law office. I'd decided on Denver because I thought it would be a fresh, clean breath of air. Back east I was inhaling what the guy in front of me exhaled. It was just a stifling atmosphere and I had a big desire to get out.

"I guess I was full of crazy ambition and had everything I needed except a wife. I didn't start needing one until Toledo, Ohio. Driving through there I stopped at a city park for a nap."

The pain killer was making him relax. He felt as if he were speaking from the edge of a dream. "Most of the time I was there I spent watching a kid wrestling under the hood of an old car. It was a '60 Chevy with a slick new paint job, bright pink. From the way that kid squirmed under the hood, I figured there wasn't anything else under there." Remembering, Irish chuckled softly. "I also figured the kid was too young to be driving, judging from the short, skinny legs sticking out. When he yelped and half-way fell onto the engine, I decided to lend a hand.

"He had the carburetor half off. Said he was trying to

clean the gas filter. I should have known no boy would yank
the carburetor without checking the battery first. The posts
were so corroded you couldn't see them. After a while it
sunk in: that skinny, little Jewish boy with all those black
curls and the navy blue eyes was really a girl!"

He moved restlessly and said, "By the time I got the carburetor back together, the terminals on the battery
cleaned, and checked out a bad wire on a spark plug, I'd
found out this Karen Palmer was driving to California to
visit an aunt.

"Talk about a babe in the woods. I tried to make her see
driving a clunk like that to California was foolish. There
were the mountains and desert ahead. But she just looked
at me as if I were the nut. From the scuffy way she was
dressed I guessed she didn't have a cent. I tried to talk her
into selling the heap and getting a plane ticket, but she became instant ice cubes and drove off."

Irish took a deep breath and tried to focus on Tina. She
was standing by the window and he couldn't see her face.
"The next place was Fort Wayne, Indiana. I recognized the
pink and white heap in front of a service station. I was
tempted to keep on going but couldn't. Curiosity, I guess.
When I got inside she was pulling a wad of bills out of her
pocket to pay for a new tire. From the size of that wad, I
guessed she was in trouble and needed to get out of town in
a hurry. That time I followed her.

"Every time she stopped for gasoline, I bought gas too
and tried to talk her into going home. All I could think of
was that delicate little imp landing in jail over that handful
of dirty bills."

For a while Irish was quiet, thinking and remembering.
He said, "We really had a good laugh about that later. She
had thought all along that I was just trying to pick her up.
She sure did her best to shake me. That's when she started
calling me 'Irish.' Said I was fighting Irish because I
wouldn't take no for an answer. I got so I could spot that car

ten miles away, almost. It was like a bright beetle darting in and out of traffic.

"We played cat and mouse across the states, and I was the cat that kept catching the mouse. There was more engine trouble and a ticket for speeding. From Peoria we dropped down to St. Louis and then she cut across to Kansas City. She was still trying to shake me. On the freeway outside of Kansas City, the pink bug died its final death.

"She had her thumb out when I caught up with her. By the time we reached Denver, I'd talked her into a marriage license. That's it."

"She sounds very independent and brave," Tina said slowly. "Doesn't she have a family?"

"Karen's father raised her. We were married six months before I found out that her father is a millionaire six times over. To listen to her, you'd think they were paupers. I still haven't figured that one out."

"What went wrong, Dan?" her voice was a whisper.

"I wish I knew. Whatever it was, it was like a creeping paralysis between us." He cleared his throat and said, "Just overnight it seemed, my beautiful little Jewish lad became a remote and tragic woman. I couldn't understand her and finally quit trying. One day there was a note and no Karen. I haven't heard from her since."

"You didn't try to find her?"

Irish only shook his head. "I suppose now she'll just want to tie up the unfinished business and be on her way. Somehow I didn't think she'd bother with divorce. Easy come, easy go. Tina, do you understand? Karen isn't a threat to me now. She's the past. At the most she'll only be an inconvenience."

Tina turned from the window. There were tears in her eyes and Irish could only watch helplessly.

"She wants to see you now."

"I suppose I must." He rolled cautiously and reached for her. She stepped back, away from him, and he said, "Tina, don't let it make a difference."

She hesitated a moment before answering and he needed to strain to hear her words. "Not a difference in how I feel, but, yes, a difference in the outcome of it all." She left the room and Irish continued to face the window, watching the clouds move past.

The door swung open again. He heard footsteps stop just inside the door. "Hi, Irish," the voice was hesitant and colorless.

"Yes, Karen," he answered, suddenly too tired to turn toward that voice. "Why have you come?"

"Because there's so much I must make right."

He puzzled over that sentence, realizing now how often he had puzzled over fragments of sentences during those last months they had been together. "That isn't necessary. The past is behind us now. Hadn't we ought to forget it? If you need money, I suppose I can give you a little. I'm about broke and I suppose I'll be living on the kindness of my clients for a few more months."

"No," her voice was sharp.

The silence between them was heavy and finally he asked, "How did you find out about the accident?"

"It was in the papers and on the news."

"Then you haven't been far away."

"No." That was all she offered and he clamped his teeth together, determined to ask no more. Beyond the window the clouds were moving faster and he continued to watch them. An occasional gust of wind pried at the window.

"Irish, I've come back."

"Oh, no you don't," he couldn't keep the bitterness out of his voice. "It's over, Karen." Now he rolled to face her, ignoring the pain that made perspiration dampen his forehead. She was standing there, three feet from the edge of the bed, grasping the chair back with rigid, defensive hands. For a long minute he studied her, trying to see in this girl the Karen he knew. He could find no resemblance to the sparkling, curly-haired imp he had first known, and little to remind him of the cool, sophisticated woman who had walked out of his life two years ago.

"What in heaven's name have you done to yourself?" His voice rasped and he watched color flood the pale cheeks beneath the overgrown brush of hair that had lost its gleam and curl. "You look like a fugitive from a bad movie."

Her dark eyes darkened more and he saw the veiled look he remembered so well. Frustration made him clench his fists under the sheet. He knew it would be impossible to reconcile his image of the Karen he had first known with this tragic, pale woman with unknowable eyes and features that seemed rigid as stone. But that was a relief. It made it possible to say the cold words.

"You can't just come back. It's over and there's no re-hashing it." He emphasized each word. "You made your choice two years ago."

Her eyes widened and she moistened her lips. "No, Irish, you don't understand. I've got to come back."

"It took you a long time to decide that."

Slowly and persistently she was shaking her head. He realized it was a bid for silence. "I must undo all the bad I've done," her voice dropped to a whisper. "Then if you no longer want me around, I'll go." He knew now that the ex-pression he was seeing in her eyes was terror. She seemed caught up in despair.

"I can't explain all this," she murmured. "I mustn't. Only just let me stay. A servant, I'll be a servant. You'll need help until you are well."

Her pleading was distasteful and it was making him im-patient. Servant. He wondered where she had picked up the word. Proud Karen, a servant?

Suddenly exhausted he shook his head and closed his eyes. "A warmed-over marriage is worse than last week's leftovers." In the next minute he heard the door close.

When it swung open again, there was Tina and two small white tablets. He tried to smile and, knowing she wouldn't ask, said, "She was ready to come back. Tina, it's completely impossible. I don't know the circumstances that brought her back. I would guess it's money, no matter what she says."

He studied Tina's face. Was he conveying the things he was feeling? These were things he couldn't put into words, but it was important for Tina to realize right now how completely uninvolved emotionally he was with Karen.

Tina was shaking her head as she held a glass of water toward him. Her face was crumpled with fatigue. "I think she was crying. I've never seen anyone look so hopeless. Dan, either she loves you deeply or she's in terrible trouble."

He moved his shoulders uneasily. "I offered her money. Tina," the words were there in spite of his resolve, "I can't be expected to shoulder her burdens again. She made her choice two years ago and if I encourage her now, she'll be a leech. Isn't it time we both go our separate ways? Even in appearance she's changed to the place I feel I no longer know her. She's a stranger."

"This whole thing is only something you and God can decide," Tina said stiffly. "It can't concern me."

"It does, and you can't deny that. Why did you say God?"

She came to the bed and stared down at him. "Dan, are you a Christian?"

"Of course. Since I was a little kid."

"I mean an honest-to-goodness, born-again kind."

"You talk as if there are degrees or varieties." He grinned up at her and reached for her hand.

"If you must put it that way, there are," she replied slowly as she pulled her hand away. A perplexed frown was on her face. "There's the book kind and—"

"Explain."

"You join a church and take all the proper classes that will merit your name being put on the right list. That's supposed to automatically mean you'll make it to heaven under the Christian banner."

"Have you a better idea?"

"God's Word says you must be born again."

"If I remember right, that's baptism."

"If it's only skin deep, no it isn't."

"When you're a child, does anything go deeper than the skin? How much deeper must it go?"

"It must," her voice was slow and deliberate, "involve all of you. When you're grasped by a great and revolutionary idea, doesn't it affect your whole life? Take being a lawyer. Doesn't it shape all of your life? Well, shouldn't the higher concept of God and man relationships influence you even more?"

"I can't see religion being in the category of a revolutionary idea."

"Perhaps you could if you were to realize the whole idea is to bring you back to your origins. The apostle Paul called it being reconciled to God."

"Back to your origins? That's evolution in reverse." He tried to act amused.

"The idea that the beginning is better than the end? Well, I guess all Christians see it that way if you go back far enough. Clear back to Adam and Eve and the original sin idea. I know it isn't modern, but personally, I'll never be convinced the present level of life is on a higher plane than the beginning."

"What about knowledge and technology?"

"What about crime and mental illness?"

"They're social ills and changeable."

"But we haven't changed them."

He grinned up at her. "Tina, I like you. I like your wholesomeness and your intelligence and I need you."

The troubled look crept across her face. "But you can't forget Karen."

"I intend to forget Karen. She's no longer my responsibility."

"You've just said she wants to come back. You said you

were a Christian. If that means you are measuring your life by Christ, you can't deny her that."

"Tina, don't go reading something into Christianity that isn't there. I want a new life."

She ignored his pointed statement. "Responsibility, it's there. God's Word is full of your responsibility to your wife. If you call yourself Christian, then you will need to accept all that it involves, won't you?"

He studied the soft contours of her face and her deeply shadowed eyes; he acknowledged the attraction they were both aware of. It was more than physical. "Then perhaps Christianity isn't that important. Not nearly as important as you are to me."

She stepped back from the bed and the soft lines of her face tightened. "Then you don't understand Christianity. Dan, you don't understand me. I am Christ's."

Five days later the doctor watched Irish walk slowly around the room with his dragging gait. "If you've arranged for nursing care, I'll dismiss you tomorrow. I just don't want you to be alone for the next couple of weeks."

Tina was standing beside the table. Irish saw her shoulders tense and then slump. She turned slowly and looked at him. Taking a deep breath full of resolve, she nodded slightly.

He knew he was grinning like a kid as he faced the doctor and he couldn't keep the triumph out of his voice. "It's all set." The doctor nodded approval and bent over the chart.

Irish looked at Tina, wondering if her decision meant the coolness of the past five days was only his imagination. She chewed at her lip and shuffled the books on the table. *It's probably only her devotion to nursing, not her devotion to me. But I'll have at least two weeks,* he reminded himself. *I can afford to go slowly.*

Chapter 4

After Karen left Irish, she stood on the steps of the hospital and watched traffic zip past. The people in the passing cars acted as if they knew where they were going, but why must they rush to get there?

Jostled, she stepped closer to the wall. The granite chilled her through the thin dress and lacy shawl. It reminded her that evening was coming and she had no place to go.

She was still trying to comprehend the fact that Irish didn't want her. Of all the thoughts and emotions she had sorted and weighed before coming back, that thought hadn't occurred to her. Now she wondered why. Why hadn't she bothered to consider how he would feel? Did the answer lie in the fact that for so long she had closed her mind to all that concerned this man whom she had married?

She wandered slowly down the steps toward the bus stop. Still in a daze she boarded the bus that would take her to the downtown apartment that had been home—their home together. Now she was passing landmarks she recognized.

She got to her feet as the bus passed the grocery store

with the green front. After the bus chugged off she walked slowly to the front of the old, red brick apartment building. Standing there she took time to study every familiar detail. She saw the pile of windswept litter where a pile had always been.

As she hesitated, wondering what had happened to the old home feeling, she noticed the child sitting on the front steps. Her nose was red with cold and she sniffed. "Hi!" The child looked the other way. Karen decided she resembled a Mulligan, but she couldn't recall her name.

Sighing she turned her attention back to the building. The street-level apartment windows were winter-streaked; she could barely see their offering of priscilla curtains and leggy geraniums. A third-story window was propped open with a pop bottle, and Karen remembered the top floors were always hot, even in early April.

Pushing the front door open, she examined the names on the mailboxes. Their apartment had a new card and she didn't recognize the name. For a moment she toyed with the idea of talking to the occupant. Another name on the mailbox caught her eye.

Marge Hanley would be home from her job at the Denver Dry's bargain basement. Karen pushed at the inner door and the familiar musty smell propelled her back in time. Slowly she mounted the steps, aware of the hurt and longing the memories were arousing.

She was thinking of the hard times they had gone through, she and Irish. There had been the burden of Irish's school bills. But there had been good times too. Even the second-hand furniture and the temperamental refrigerator had been fun because they had been part of home. Together and alone had been the nicest part. For a long time a hamburger by candlelight had been heaven.

If only, she thought wistfully, *Irish had been satisfied with things as they were. Why couldn't he accept me like I was instead of insisting I have a career too.?*

That was when the trouble began. "Fulfillment," "challenge," he had called it. She shuddered and, lost in thought, wondered what there had been about her that wasn't complete enough for him.

It couldn't have had anything to do with the young attorneys he associated with. They had been poor too, with their babies and shabby apartments. Irish hadn't seemed to mind the shabby apartment, but he had been firm about not wanting babies. Her mind slid away from that.

There was that secret feeling she had always had about Irish's driving ambition. Somehow she sensed, even in the beginning, Irish had wanted to prove himself better than any other attorney in Denver. He would count no sacrifice too great. The old familiar bitterness threatened her.

In an attempt to be fair, she focused her attention on the Irish who had grown up in New York City. Again she felt the familiar ache for that little boy. She knew he had been raised a stranger to the things she had always taken for granted. It wasn't the love and laughter, because he seemed to have had that, but instead nourishing food and warm clothing.

Irish had talked about his mother until Karen felt she could close her eyes and see the stocky woman with her red-gray hair and laundry-reddened arms. Certainly Irish had made Karen feel the affection and love he held for his mother, and never had he been ashamed of her just because she had spent her life cleaning houses for other women.

Dear Irish. She yearned over the picture of the thin little redhead, abandoned by his father, bewildered and lonely on the streets of New York. But with such a mother, how could he be less than the best lawyer in Denver?

Karen's feet dragged on the stairs as she started up the last flight. Thinking about Irish's home made her feel guilty—guilty for always having had so much and appreciating it so little.

What would it have been like to have that sturdy woman squeeze her tightly when she came home from school? And maybe kiss and tuck her in at night? She felt her lips lift in a cozy smile. What silly childish thoughts.

Marge's door was ajar. She took a moment to muster her courage, to summon that bright, happy Karen. "Hey, Marge," she tapped and shouted in the familiar old way. "Gotta spare bed?"

"Well, Karen St Clair, I'll be hanged for a witch yet. I conjured you! I've been thinking and thinking about you. You poor little waif, get in here!"

Marge waved one hand with its cigarette and the other with the coffee cup. She turned and padded into the living room. "Plop and I'll get you some java. Where you been?"

She returned with the coffee and pushed aside a pile of magazines to make room for Karen. "The saints are good to me. Let me look at you. You're still the same little washed-out prune under all that hair." She lifted the shawl from Karen's shoulders and peered critically at the rumpled muslin.

"You gone far east or something? You look about like the oddballs on the street. That's a pretty far cry from the neat little product Freddie made you out to be. What's up?"

"Irish doesn't live here anymore?" Marge shook her head as she took a long drag on her cigarette.

She squinted her eyes and appraised Karen. "No, moved out just before he had that bad accident. I don't know where he's gone. I suppose I could ask around for you.

"He turned into a real snob after you left. Wouldn't have a thing to do with us all. I guess he just tolerated us all along because his wife didn't have sense enough to stay away from the scum of the earth."

"Oh, Marge, you know better than that. You've been the dearest friend a person could have. I'd, well, I just wouldn't have made it those last months if it hadn't been for you."

"Yeah, I made you laugh when you felt like crying. Some help. But you sure took out of here when you finally decided to go. I take it there was a final straw?" Her eyes were bright with curiosity but Karen shook her head.

"Marge, do you mind? I still can't talk about it."

"Sure, honey, I don't mean to pry. It's plain to see you're worse off now than you were before."

Karen's hands went to her face. "Oh, no, that isn't possible. It's just that I can't seem to really find myself."

"What's with the garb?"

"Oh, nothing much. I've been living at a commune and everyone else dressed like this. It's pretty easy to be just like the rest of them."

"How come a commune?"

"Well, I suppose it started out like the line of least resistance. I needed something badly and the only ones who seemed interested in helping me were all headed for this commune. They took me along."

"What was it like?"

She shrugged, unable to sort out the important things. "Just free and easy. The only thing they ask is that you do your share of the work. That was simple."

"Why are you back? You and Irish going to make another try of it?"

She shook her head, "No. Marge, I don't know whether or not you'll understand this, but I've started meditating. Up there they all do it and they made me realize it's the only really progressive way to live." Marge blew a skeptical smoke ring. "It's kinda' like religion. You learn how to live in a way that releases you to God."

"Shouldn't think you'd have to take off to a commune to learn that."

"But I did. I wish I could express myself in a way to make you really understand, Marge. It's all wonderful. I always thought God was such a terrible thing, just waiting to pounce on you when you do wrong. And I feel like I'm always doing wrong. Up there they said He's good and kind and judging isn't His business at all. All He does is help make it possible for you to live right. It's all so simple. You get that way not by trying but just by being. You put yourself in a position of surrender to Him. You let yourself be in Him. Marge, you just automatically do good when you're in that position."

Marge's eyebrows raised and Karen protested, "Don't look like that. It isn't anything spooky or such. You don't feel a thing. You just have to believe and not expect sensation."

"So what's the point in all that?"

"You mean why? To spread good. To help others learn how to meditate so that we can all get to the place where we create happiness and serenity and have peace. That's the only way we can finally escape this trap."

"What trap?" Marge asked.

Karen saw the bewilderment on Marge's face and realized how little she was communicating. "Well," she said slowly, "it's this having to do it all over and over again until we can escape the influence of karma and finally merge with God."

"Sounds like reincarnation," Marge snorted. "Karen, you don't believe in that! Come on, let's get some dinner into you and talk sensibly."

Frustrated, Karen tried again. "I've done this enough to be convinced that it is the only way. Marge, meditating is wonderful. All the tension and unhappiness evaporates. Even when you come back into everyday life, you are able to cope with it better. The ultimate is to be so into it that you can take that state with you all the time."

"And you're there?"

"No, that's why I've come back. Marge, the karma of the past is ruining everything. They told me I had to go back and make it right, now while I'm still able to. If I don't, then generations and generations from now someone will be suffering terribly because of my failure to create good to those around me. I didn't treat Irish right. I could have been a more loving wife. Besides," she shut her eyes tightly for a moment, "I just can't stand the thought of someone else having to go through what I've been going through. I can make it right. I know I can if Irish will only give me a chance."

"You act to me like you have a guilty conscience." Karen's hand went slowly to her throat. "You been taking drugs and shacking up with someone?"

"Oh, Marge," she studied the face that had suddenly become cold and impersonal. She found she could hardly force her voice above a whisper. "No, never. I have enough problems without adding to them by doing things like that. Besides, they don't allow things like that up there. If you want to be successful with meditating, you've got to live a decent life. That's part of my trouble. There's stuff in the past I've got to get over or I'll never be able to do it right." She ignored the question marks she saw in Marge's eyes.

"So you're here to spread peace and love to Irish. What does he think of it all?"

"He doesn't want it. But he's got to let me come back. The consequences will be terrible if he doesn't, and not just to me but to him too. I don't like coming back to this mess. It's like facing a bad dream. I'm not staying a moment longer than I have to."

"Meanwhile, you don't have a place to sleep, right? Well, baby, you're welcome to stay here. Somehow I don't think you're going to have much success. Karen, honey, I hate to see you hurt more. You were always too loyal to level about life with the Red Baron, but I've got the idea he really put you through it. I don't want to see you looking like living death again. Please, baby, when it's rough again, come to Marge instead of splitting."

The tears welled up in Karen's eyes. She blinked and said, "You're the dearest friend a person could ever have."

"Naw, you just yank the heart out of a body. Now come on, let's have some of that soup."

The next morning they were still talking over cooling cups of coffee when Karen suddenly became aware of time. "Marge, I've made you late for work."

Marge put down her coffee cup and studied Karen. "I'm not going," she said. "I've worked for that place for twenty years and it's about time I tell them when I'm not coming to work. I called and I said, 'There's this little gal who needs to talk. I may be in today and I may not.'"

"Oh, Marge," Karen felt as if her heart were sinking into her sandals.

"Yeah, I know. You're thinking 'That Marge'll put the thumb screws on me and I'll have to talk.' Karen, I don't want no true confession. I happen to believe you when you said you'd been living it straight, but I got this feeling you'd like to do a little thinking out loud. I'm here to prod you on with the 'then whats.'"

But Karen sat dumb, tied in the knots of the past, knowing that whatever she tried to say wouldn't be easy.

"I know all about you and Irish meeting on that trip out here and how you fell in love and got married before you had good sense. Karen, I don't think divorce is bad. Sometimes it's the only way. My old man and me, we just couldn't make it. I just wanted to run to that divorce court like it would solve all my problems. It doesn't. I don't know why, but you never really shake off a marriage. It just makes you into something that never seems to change back into what you were before, no matter how single you feel."

"Marge, I'm not talking about divorce. In fact, I hadn't thought of it at all. I suppose Irish will want it someday, and that's his responsibility. I wish I could make you understand all this."

Karen got to her feet and began clearing the breakfast things from the table. The little window over the sink emitted a neat square of sunshine that warmed the white porcelain of the sink and gave a homey glow to the flowered china.

While Marge finished her cigarette and the now luke-warm coffee, Karen filled the dishpan with suds and lifted the dishes slowly and carefully. She shook back her hair and savored the clean white of her surroundings.

"It's nice to have running hot water and clean white enamel. We had an old wood-burning range and a splintery table."

"Why did you go to that place?"

Karen recognized the threatening 'then whats' and said slowly, "It really happened just as I said it did. These kids picked me up. I didn't have any place to go, so I just tagged along."

"You could have come here."

Her voice was husky, "I couldn't. I had to leave."

"You could have kicked him out. You had a nice set up and a good job."

"I had to run."

"You're different, all the way through. Before, you laughed and cried. Karen, you lived high and low, but at least you lived. Now, it's like I can't touch you."

Karen turned from the sink to look at Marge. The woman's steady dark eyes seemed to penetrate the differences, the dress and hair. Idly Karen wondered if she glimpsed anything that reminded her of the old Karen. She hoped not. That would be a chink in the armor.

"I can guess. You don't want me to see the old Karen or the new. Hey, kid, that's okay. You have your rights to a secret life."

There was silence in the kitchen while Karen finished the dishes, wiped the table and counters and then came to sit with Marge, to listen, as she said, "Do you remember Dorothy Mulligan?"

"Yes, I thought I recognized one of her children on the steps last night."

Marge nodded. "Remember how I used to pester her,

kept trying to get her to open up? You can't help a body if they won't let you. Well, she died. I knew all along that she was having deep troubles with that old man and everything, but I couldn't get next to her. Well, she did herself in. Jumped off the bridge in front of a train."

"And you're thinking I'm the same way. Well, Marge, you're wrong. I'm not having troubles like that."

"Then why are you back with that strange garb and those scary eyes? Karen, I don't know what there is about us humans that makes going it twice as hard when we're going it alone."

The next day Karen talked. Unexpectedly, overflowing and at a nonstop rush. She had been listening to Marge. For the third time, Marge had called Irish the Red Baron. From her tranquil position on the floor, with folded hands and crossed legs, Karen flew upward.

"Marge, will you stop calling Irish that horrible name! You don't understand him. All you saw was what you wanted to see and he wasn't like that at all."

Marge blinked, hesitated and then settled deeper in her chair. "Well, then what do you want me to believe? That life was all heaven in that third-floor apartment? Karen, I saw the life drain out of you. I watched you become nothing more than a shadow around him."

"But Marge, that wasn't all his fault." Her voice dropped to a whisper, "No matter how bad the whole affair became, I can't let you blame him for it all."

She settled back on to the floor and delved back into memory, putting words to the feelings that had lain hidden for so long.

"Partly it was immaturity on my part. I was looking for something that couldn't be found in Irish."

She went to sit on the couch beside Marge. "Do you suppose a person could subconsciously be searching for some link? Oh, I know I'm saying this all badly. But now, looking back, I almost feel as if I tried to use Irish to take the place of. . . . This is ridiculous." She stopped for a moment and then said, "Well, of God. You know, I really adored him. He was the most perfectly wonderful human alive. Perhaps if I hadn't felt that way, then maybe—well, when I found he had clay feet, it wouldn't have been so devastating.

"Marge, I wish I could find the words to let you know how I really felt. There was so much security, a coming-home feeling with Irish. And it was to a home that I didn't know existed. I just gave myself totally to the whole thing—marriage. I guess that's why coming back to earth and reality was so much worse. For a short time it was really ideal. He needed me and I needed him. More than that, we were each other's completed self and it was heaven. I didn't know the possibility of fulfillment existed in another person."

"And you came down to earth when you found out he was human," Marge said dryly. "Karen, are you telling me that you left Irish because you discovered that he wasn't perfect?" Marge stood up and moved restlessly around her little apartment. "You've got to live with reality, and reality is dirty socks and a husband who doesn't know you exist except when he's hungry."

"No, Marge, I'm saying it all wrong. I didn't mean a perfect person." She was silent for a moment and then the words burst out impatiently, "But why is there this desire, this dream of the ideal, of perfection, hovering around marriage, there but just a touch away from us? So near you can almost grasp it." She slumped. "I guess we would be content with reality if it weren't for that feeling that there's something better just beyond our reach."

For a long time Karen studied her coffee cup, swishing the dregs around its sides and then she looked up. "You can't think I'd go through that heartbreak simply because he was imperfect. Oh, Marge, leaving him was the most horrible thing I've ever gone through. I didn't know separation would do that to a person. I thought it would be like it was before. I thought that after the lonelines was gone, I would still be a whole person, but I'm—I mean, I wasn't."

Finally Karen looked up. Marge's face was crumpled with sorrow and fatigue. She knew the expression was an echo of her own feelings, the ones buried just beneath the surface. "Don't look that way," she pleaded. "All this talk has accomplished nothing except to make you feel the hurts again."

"That's the thing they don't tell us when they say divorce is wrong. They can't show us the wounds that are left. You don't get over it, babe. It's been sixteen years since me and my old man called it quits. You don't heal. You just get thick scars over the holes. If we hadn't been so stubborn . . . well, never mind. What's done is done."

Marge headed for the kitchen. "How about a sandwich?" Karen nodded without enthusiasm and trailed along behind Marge. After pulling bread and cheese from the refrigerator, Marge picked up a long knife and, carefully inspecting its edge, asked, "But how about you and Irish? Can't you do something before it's too late?"

Karen picked up the plates. "No, Marge, there's no way to go back."

"But why? I can't be convinced there was enough to really break you two up."

Satisfied with the knife, Marge uncovered the cheese, "Unless there's more to the story." The knife bit into the cheese and she lifted a quizzical eyebrow.

"There's more, Marge, but I can't talk about it." Karen realized her voice was quivering and she got hastily to her feet. "May I bring you another cup of coffee?"

Marge nodded and Karen felt her eyes as she bent over the coffee pot. "Don't ask more," she whispered, passing the cup to Marge. "I can't take it."

"Well, I won't, but I'm sure convinced you're still interested in that guy. That seems like a good enough reason to try again."

"Do you know, Marge? I have something better now. Marriage isn't necessary. I've found a reason for living that transcends marriage." Her hands touched the muslin of her dress in an unconsciously revealing way.

"You're talking about your far-east ideas," Marge said slowly. "I'd guessed maybe they were having some deep effect on you. At first I was afraid this deal with Irish had done something to your mind to the place that you were on your way to being a real zombie. But that's not it, is it?"

"No, Marge," Karen smiled now. "That's a funny way to put it, but what you are seeing is the peace and tranquillity of my life now compared to what I was when Irish and I lived together. I wouldn't trade the peace I have for marriage."

"But you've come back."

"We believe that it is our duty to permeate all of life with this message of peace. Everyone must have it."

"Well, it will sure take care of the population explosion if you succeed with all your teaching," Marge said dryly.

Karen sighed and shook her head. "No, you've failed to understand. There's no call to an ascetic life. People are expected to go on living as they always have. It's just that the practice of meditation lifts you up to a mental state that helps make all of your physical living take place on a higher plane."

"But you and Irish. It's pretty lonely, this being without someone. I wouldn't wish that on you, not if there is some possibility of change."

"Change? Yes, but not what you think. Marge, I hadn't intended to push these ideas off on you. My beliefs, I mean. But when I see your misery, I've got to do something to help you. Please don't try to shove Irish and me back together again. I really don't want it. I know that never again in this life will I want that type of relationship. Perhaps later, way down the line, but not while I'm still Karen. See, what I've gained through meditation more than makes up for what I've lost in marriage. I realize now that I was trying to make

Irish fill the role of God, make him be my peace and tranquillity and total love. But he wasn't up to the job. He judged everything I did, from the way I cooked eggs to the way I dressed. Now I'm beyond ever being hurt by his criticism." She stopped to take a deep breath and stated deliberately and slowly, "The tranquillity of my life is real because it's totally wrapped up in meditation. I will not let him disturb me again."

"It sounds to me like you've built a wall around yourself and refuse to feel anything." Marge was emphasizing the words. She paused long enough to reach for cigarettes and matches. "You can't live that way forever. Your phony shell will crack."

Serenely, confidently, Karen lifted her chin. "No, Marge, you're wrong. Total peace is not an illusion. It's the other human emotions that we've lived with for so long that are illusions, the fear and guilt. They are emotions that we must rise above.

"Marge, life really is beautiful, but you must learn how to experience it in a beautiful way. This city, the noise and confusion and dirt, the pushing and rudeness and brutality must be overcome.

"The mountains are an almost perfect picture of how life should be. I would like to stay up there forever, but instead I must learn how to bring the mountains down to me. I close my eyes and concentrate on a perfect scene. This way." Karen folded her hands and rested her head against the back of the chair. "It's early morning. The sun is a deep red-gold arch beyond the trees and mountain peaks. The color turns the snowy peaks behind me to pure gold. The wild flowers and tall meadow grass are heavy with dew; they droop and press their burden of moisture on me as I walk. I hear the family sounds of birds. They are contented and safe. Tiny animals move slowly away from me as I go. They too seem unafraid, caught in the loving magic of early morning. The scent of it all is as love must smell—sharp and pungent, heady and warm. Now the water crashes down the mountain, rushing over rocks and the sound makes me thirsty. There is nothing more soul satisfying than that icy water. I think it comes directly from heaven, still full of the taste of snow. I—'' Her eyes popped open. Marge was nodding with a cynical expression that bounced Karen back to earth.

"And there's the jolt back to real life. Karen, I'm not convinced that escape is good. Couldn't it get to be so attractive that you end up spending more time escaping than living?"

"And what is true living but escaping to that far country?" She got to her feet. "Marge, you scoff now, but remember what I've told you. Some day you must come into this way of life. We all must. That's why I'm back. I'm passionately committed to the task of educating others to this."

Her fingers curled tightly around each other and her voice dropped to a throaty whisper. "I don't want to be Irish's wife, but almost I think I'd be willing to die if he would embrace this wonderful way of living. Do you understand? Meditation is the door to experiencing life to its fullest. Don't we all want that?"

Marge's troubled eyes searched Karen's as she put her coffee cup down. "But you don't look fulfilled. You look like you're hiding under the covers. And you don't look serene. You look like you swallowed a couple of sleeping pills."

Karen sighed with exasperation and got to her feet. "Something tells me this spreading the message is going to be a bigger task than I thought."

Chapter 5

The ambulance was part of the doctor's final orders. But at the door of the elevator in the condominium, even Tina sided with Irish. "He can make it on his own now." Her voice was crisp and professional.

The elevator was swift and silent. Irish followed Tina slowly while she herded the ambulance attendant with his load of books and plants. At his own front door, they broke rank and silently waited. The crocheted bundle in front of the door moved and Karen stood up. "Sorry," she murmured, "I've waited awhile." The attendant arched an eyebrow and Tina turned to Irish. Irish sighed and pushed the key into the lock.

While the attendant carried the drooping chrysanthemum into the dining room and the books to the bedroom, Irish stood in the middle of the chrome and glass, the fur and leather, and swayed miserably. Karen turned slowly in the middle of the room. "It's so," her navy blue eyes were troubled. He could guess the questions. Money. Where did it come from? Turning he headed down the hall.

Tina was waiting beside his bedroom door. She avoided his eyes and he knew the problems of the previous week were still unresolved. He leaned heavily against the door-jamb. "Get rid of her."

Tina's head jerked and her eyes widened with disbelief. "Rid of her!" She repeated. He saw contempt growing on her face as she slowly asked, "And you don't care what happens to her, do you? Does she have money, a place to stay?" Wearily he closed his eyes. "Dan, she's your responsibility."

Under the rush of words the idea grew. "Wait," he reached for her arm. "There's the other bedroom and twin beds. If she stays, it would solve the live-in arrangement my nurse wouldn't agree to, wouldn't it?" Her eyes were still cold, but she nodded briefly and turned quickly toward the living room. It was almost, Irish thought, as if she expected him to change his mind again.

Karen counted the days. It had been a week since she had moved into Irish's life again. Tina and Irish were still treating her like an outsider, only a tolerated guest. She told herself she didn't really mind too much, but underneath she had a deep desire to give up on the whole project and go back to the commune. Then she reminded herself that she must conquer the past now or there could be no future.

Sitting in the middle of the giant leather pouf in Irish's living room, she shoved thought aside and tried to meditate. The whisper of that white uniform moving back and forth was a blazing thrust of distraction.

Karen struggled for serenity and nothingness. There was the word. The pushing of her mind away from thought was like pushing a canoe away from shore. Drift. Swish, swish—that was the uniform. That tinkle was glass against glass.

Was Irish still that weak? Or was he avoiding her by staying in that room? She peeked. Only five minutes had passed. With a sigh she gave up the idea of meditating just now and got up.

Sunlight was pouring through the wall of windows. Each

neat rectangle of light rested on an object, illuminating it all as if the room were a giant display case. She thought the leather couch with its fur pillows should have been on a rotating dais. Karen acknowledged the tasteful blends of cinnamon, off-white and black which dominated the room; but the too perfect, stage-like quality of the room made her want to throw pillows. She looked around the room, searching for some hint of real life.

Tina was coming; she could hear her swish. As Karen turned and waited, she tried to analyze the nurse. Tina seemed cold. Her carefully arranged blonde curls and too perfect features made Karen think of an animated china doll.

She found herself discarding her opinion when she saw Tina's obvious nervousness as the nurse came into the room. The hand she stretched toward Karen trembled.

"Dan wants you to have this." Tina pressed crumpled bills into Karen's hands. "He says you're to buy clothes."

"I don't need any." She couldn't keep the scorn out of her voice. "I have this and jeans."

It was easy to see Tina was embarrassed. She hesitated for a moment and Karen couldn't understand her expression and indecision. "Karen," she spoke carefully, "I have no right to tell you what to do. You're Dan's wife and I'm only a hired nurse, but—"

"Oh," Karen shook her head, "you misunderstand. I *was* his wife. I've come back only long enough to help him, not to be his wife again."

Tina frowned. Looking at Karen's hair, the long muslin dress, and her bare feet, she said, "You've come back. Isn't that an indication you want to continue your life as it was before?"

"I don't think people really go back, only forward. I don't know that for a fact. Someday, perhaps, I'll ask the guru."

"But you're here."

"Not to be as I was, but to mend the trouble I caused and then to go on." Tina looked bewildered and Karen let her turn away. Looking at the wad of bills, Karen saw there was over a hundred dollars. "May I see Irish?"

"Of course. He's your husband."

Karen moved her head impatiently and walked down the hall. Irish's bedroom was decorated in cherry red, her favorite color. Before, in that old place, she had used the color in their bedroom. She shrugged off the memories and looked at Irish. He was reading in bed. The bed wasn't the same one. This one was oversized.

Impatient with her thoughts, she quickly walked to the bed and thrust the bills at him. "I don't need clothes."

He looked over the book. Even under the red beard she could see the hard line of his jaw. "If you insist on staying here, you'll have to have them."

"If it is the dress that offends you," she was snapping the words in a way she hadn't used since leaving him, "I'll wear the blue jeans. That's the universal uniform."

He was looking at her hair. "You've forgotten," she continued, trying to control her voice, "I didn't come back as your wife. I've told you I've only come back to undo the wrong I've done. I must bring you serenity and happiness, love and peace."

His eyes were hard. *They are like the guru's ring*, she thought, *the hard, cold emerald. That's why I didn't like that ring. It's the color of Irish's hating look.*

Irish dropped his book and looked at her. "It doesn't work, does it?" he knew his voice was cold with the contempt he was feeling. "Love, happiness? Karen, don't labor the point. Let's just find our happiness in going our separate ways. You made the choice two years ago. I'd like to make my choice now."

Irish watched the effect of his words. Since the shock of her visit to the hospital, he had found himself remembering and contrasting the Karens he had known. The high-spirited girl with the pink car had been an eager, happy bride. In the beginning the career woman had been confident and determined. When had she become brittle?

He admitted that dwelling on the memory of their life together was painful and bewildering, but he also acknowledged that during the past two years he had discovered every moment that wasn't crammed with work and study had been filled with a constant procession of life in review. He had searched each scene, looking for clues that would explain the breakdown in their marriage. The evidences of breakdown were there. The reasons still eluded him.

Now as he watched Karen, he was tempted to ask, but that was a step backward he wasn't willing to take.

He could see the effect his statement was having on her. When she had first marched into the room, her face had been rigid and expressionless. During his silent scrutiny, the mask had slipped. Nervously she chewed at her lip. He watched her press clenched fists against her stomach.

Impatiently he said, "Every time I've looked at you, you've been grabbing your middle. Do you have an ulcer?"

She looked at him with startled eyes. "No." She hesitated, turned and left the room.

He was still working his way out of bed when he heard the front door close.

Tina was in the living room with a magazine. He took a deep breath and tried to forget his anger and frustration before he entered the room. Tina looked over the magazine and asked, "She's left?"

"I hope forever. It'll never work and I can't understand her trying again. She's a mature person, well able to make a new life for herself."

"She doesn't appear that way." Tina thumbed through the magazine. "She comes across as immature and very bewildered. Why the robe? Has she always dressed in this off-beat way?"

Irish looked up from his careful pacing of the floor. "No. Karen's," he tried to find the words, "well, she's always looked like every other woman on the street."

"Can she really take care of herself?"

"Yes, she's proven that. I was very proud of her position. About six months after we were married, she decided she wanted a career. Of course, I urged her to go ahead. She's only had two years of college and I think that was the reason she did a good deal of fumbling around before she found a situation she could grow in. But after she found it, she did a fantastic job. I believe she could have been really successful if she'd only stuck with it."

"What did she do?" Tina piled pillows in a chair and patted the arm.

Irish shook his head, "No, thanks. I'm more comfortable on my feet. Karen worked as an apprentice to a fashion designer. She had quite a flair for the unique in line and color. I pulled a few strings and got her accepted as a girl Friday with a design and modeling agency here in Denver. Of course, it's nothing to compare with what you'd find back east, but it was an up and coming company. They did a lot for her. Almost overnight she matured into a really sophisticated woman." That's also when Karen had become remote, his memory prodded him.

"And she just suddenly left you in the middle of all that success?" Tina's voice was filled with question marks.

He turned to look at her. "Either you don't think it's success, or perhaps you're indicating I was unaware. Listen, Tina, we were close. She was anxious to please." Quietly he thought about that word. "Anxious" was the key, anxious and tense, with strained white lips that had forgotten to smile and anxiety-filled eyes.

"Look," he mentally shook himself free of the picture, "in the bottom drawer of the sideboard in the dining room is a portfolio of Karen's drawings." Tina looked surprised and Irish needed to explain. "I hated to throw them out. They could be valuable."

"The way fashion changes?" Tina went to the dining room. Thumbing through the folder, she came back and slowly sat down. In silence she turned over every drawing while Irish peered over her shoulder and then paced the floor.

"They are good. They're fantastically good," Tina said slowly. "I don't know a thing about fashion or art, but these things appeal to me in a surprising way."

"And that could explain why Freddie tried to con me out of the set just after Karen left." Silently he paced again.

Tina returned the folder to the drawer and came back into the living room. "I guess," Irish said thoughtfully, "she did work too hard. It seemed those last few months she was constantly carrying a stack of magazines or drawings. Sometimes I had the feeling the head woman, Freddie, was a real work horse. At least I have the impression she was constantly whipping the others into line."

"You said fashion design, but you make it sound more like a sweat factory."

He stopped his pacing and looked at her. "Yes," he said slowly, feeling his way with words, "I guess the essence of it all is that regardless of the trappings, contentment is a necessary ingredient in any job."

"And Karen was content?"

"Of course." He felt he was trying to convince himself.

"If she were all that well adjusted, how could she change so much?"

"Why does anyone change? Boredom? Tina, I don't know. I've asked myself the same question over and over."

"And now you're throwing up your hands ready to quit."

"Tina, why should I hang in there when it's all over?"

"She's come back."

"But not because she wants to be my wife. She wants nothing except to spread peace and love and then be on her way."

"And you won't let her."

"I'm not stopping her. It's this strange hang-up she has.

The whole situation gives me the creeps." He walked to Tina and looked down at her. "That clothes bit. I gathered she'd been living the hippy life, and I figured she didn't have anything decent to wear. It turns out that she can't see any reason to look presentable. That's not the Karen I knew before."

"But what are you going to do now?"

"Hope she does her thing and leaves." He knew his voice was hard. He watched Tina avert her face.

The front door opened and closed. As Tina and Irish waited, they heard a rustle of paper from the kitchen. There was the running of water and a pop as if the refrigerator door was opened and closed. Irish shrugged and rolled his eyes at Tina. The sounds continued and Irish paced the floor.

"I'd better check," Tina murmured and headed for the kitchen. Irish followed. Karen was shaking water from a pile of greens.

"I'm cooking tonight," she said tersely. The silence seemed to give her courage. "Since I've been here," she continued, "Irish has lain in bed, Tina has swished back and forth, and I've done nothing. From now on, I'll do the cooking."

"That too?" Irish pointed to the greenery in a large clay pot.

"That's dieffenbachia. The living room's too bare. Will you put it to the left of the windows? It should have plenty of sunlight." Irish reached for the pot.

Tina swooped down on the pot. "Your back! I'll take it." She paused and turned to Karen. Irish noticed there was a slight edge to her voice as she asked, "Do you want to learn all about therapy too?"

"No," Karen answered serenely, "that's your territory."

"I'm sorry," Tina muttered. "That was childish." She brushed past Irish with the plant.

"What's this?" he prodded the greens with his finger.

"Watercress. I'm going to make a spinach pie for dinner. Know what's good? French fried parsnips."

"I'd rather have steak and potatoes."

She looked up at him with a perplexed frown. "I didn't think of that." Her eyes slowly widened and she said, "But maybe that's all the trouble, wrong food. You see, you must eat right to get the right vibes. I've been doing this for so long I'd forgotten you didn't know. Steak and potatoes are okay I guess, but this is better."

He frowned down at her earnest face, aware of a frustrating need to understand. "Karen, what is this? What strange thing has happened to you to make you act like a different person? You dress like—" he waved his hands helplessly.

"Do you really want to know," she asked slowly, "or are you only wanting to pick at me again. You see, Irish, you mustn't. I can't take it, the poking at all that's most important to me."

"You've never said I attacked you in that way. What is important? Surely you don't mean this?" he gestured toward the greens on the counter and her dress.

She turned away from him. Her shoulders drooped and the fuzz of her hair was a shield before her face. "That hair, you look like a porcupine."

"I wish it had barbs. Why are humans so defenseless?" He couldn't answer, but he continued to lean against the counter and watch as she worked.

The next day Karen was in the kitchen when the telephone rang. She recognized the voice immediately, and it was as if the two years had disappeared. Totally unprepared for the emotional shock she was feeling, she leaned against the wall and moistened her lips before replying, "Freddie, how did you know I'd come back?"

The hearty voice boomed in her ear, fascinating and repelling. She closed her eyes and the woman's presence was as vivid as if that lanky, six-foot frame were in the kitchen with her. The voice demanded an answer.

"No, I'm not coming back to the studio. I'm leaving here when Irish is better." She took a deep breath and fought for courage to say, "I won't be in, Freddie. This is better. I have no intention of renewing old acquaintances."

She gently replaced the receiver, surprised at her unexpected bravery. As she waited for her pulse to slow, she thought about the studio and Freddie. The memories were disquieting, painful, but never had she supposed they could throw her into this emotional upheaval.

She pushed away from the wall, wishing she could as easily push away from that engulfing personality. "But," she muttered to herself, "that's one reason why I've come back, to forever silence all the old memories that won't let me be a whole person. And, Karen," she remonstrated, "be honest. Freddie couldn't have been responsible. She suggested, but you went to that clinic of your own free will."

She walked unsteadily to the sink and dabbed at the scouring powder scattered there. The deeply buried memories had surfaced and she could only gently probe the spots that were tender, unhealed wounds. When could she convince herself? When did guilt cease being guilt?

Karen heard Tina's key in the lock and gratefully hurried to the door. She took the packages and said, "Irish is sleeping."

Thoughtfully Tina studied her face as she slowly pulled off her gloves. "Why do you call Dan Irish?"

"He's fighting Irish. But I never realized how true to his real nature that nickname is. He's a fighter, not a lover. There's nothing soft and warm and needing in Irish."

Tina didn't reply, but Karen sensed her surprise at that last comment.

Karen sat in the middle of the cinnamon and black rya rug centered in the stream of sunlight. She deliberately focused on the task of releasing the tension in her arms. *I wish I could relax the wound-tight steel spring inside*, she thought, trying to concentrate on the limpness of her arms.

"What are you doing?" Her eyes flew open. Irish stood in the doorway. He looked unusually tired and she guessed it was pain.

"Meditating. You should try it. It would help the pain." He snorted and moved impatiently around the room. "But you're not open to anything except Irish's way, are you?"

"That's what you call serenity and love?" He turned in that stiff-necked way she remembered so well. Anger drew a white line of tension along his nostrils.

Like abstract pictures, distorted by time, she was remembering those other occasions when his anger had flared, scathing her. *But then*, she reminded herself from that remote, untouchable position she had willed for herself, *I was so vulnerable. To be in love is to have no defense against burning, cutting anger. To not be in love is power and control. To not be in love with Irish is strength that will never subject me to hurt again.*

He was speaking and she drifted away from the shelter of her thoughts to hear him. "That statement implies you were the perfect little wife, the long-suffering love-slave. Don't try to impress me with your virtues. After all, you were the one who left."

"And are you without blame?" She was coolly aware of her remote, passionless voice and was beginning to enjoy the sharp thrust of her words.

"Irish, I didn't run away from home. I left an unbearable situation. I left you."

His anger flushed his face. "Because you weren't woman enough to create a marriage? It was easier, Karen, wasn't it, to just run out when the going was rough? How lightly you hold relationships. Did you skip out on another fellow when it got stormy? Is that really why you've come back?"

Like a burst of sudden fire, Karen felt the coldness melt. She rushed across the room and on tiptoe she screamed up at Irish. "You think I am that kind of person? Remember, Irish, remember what it was like in the beginning? Did you think I was pretending the love? Could I have offered that to anyone else?"

Abruptly the anger faded and she watched heavy lines rumple his face. She could scarcely hear his voice. "No, Karen, no matter what, I could never believe you to be that kind of person."

It was the time to push those past hurts out to the surface, but in the face of his defeat she couldn't. For a moment longer she watched, overwhelmed by the memories that could almost block out the bad times.

"What went wrong, Karen?"

Dully, "Is it possible to believe that it was a total of everything? Can angry shouting and bitter words become a way of life that leaves no room for the gentle emotions?"

He was intently studying her face. She felt the need for retreat, but she steeled herself against it. *I will be strong,* she told herself. *I won't let him force me into running again.*

"Karen, that wasn't it. The deadness between us started long before the shouting did. And there wasn't all that much shouting, if you remember. Did you know I felt as if I were trying to shout down a wall? Your Jericho." His face twisted in a painful grin. "Well?"

She bit her lip and stared at the rug.

His voice came impatient and cold, "End of conversation, right? That's the way it always was." After another silent moment he left the room.

Alone Karen tried again to spiral down into that deep part. The thoughts wouldn't push away. Karma. They said at the commune that her problem with meditating was all the bad karma and it was up to her to change it all.

"Spread love where you've spread hate, spread peace where you've spread strife, spread good where you've spread evil," she recited. She stopped and bent over the rug.

They said it was possible, but more and more she was

discovering it was not, at least not yet. How, she wondered, do you change the unchangeable, create good out of a horrible evil when there is no going back?

There was the memory of that one, unchangeable deed. Even now it was engulfing her like a black cloud, and yet she felt like a spectator. *It's like*, she thought, *in the deepest part of me I can't really acknowledge that horrible person is me.* She recalled that they had said, "Deny it all. Evil is from gross karma and that no longer exists for you now that you are meditating."

"Are you ready for your back rub?" Irish dropped the book and nodded to Tina. She helped him out of the brace and he rolled over.

"Tina, did you know Karen is meditating? Does that possess some strange hold over a person?"

"If you believe the advertisements you hear," she murmured, "it's only a simple and harmless mental exercise that enables you to get more out of life. I don't know anything about it."

"She's become strange," he said slowly. "It's as if she's in tune with two worlds at once. She acts as if she can no longer laugh or cry in this world."

"Is it possible she's having psychological problems of some sort?" Tina asked, "Perhaps she's been deeply hurt."

"Tina, why do I keep feeling as if you're making jabs at me? A marriage is two people's responsibility. Karen has stepped out of her half and I can no longer feel responsible for her."

"Did you at one time have a deep sense of responsibility for her?" Tina asked the question as if it was forced from her and Irish rolled over. Her face was troubled. "I mean, going beyond the physical into the emotional?"

"Until now I've always considered Karen completely normal."

"Then what can explain her present situation?" Tina

cried. "Dan, I'm not picking on you. I'm trying to understand this strange woman, and mostly because I feel personally involved in the whole affair."

Irish extended his hand, touched hers. "What affair? You won't let there be anything except this patient-nurse relationship."

"It must be that way, Dan. I can't afford to let myself be involved before I can see where it all leads."

"But you are a little involved?"

"A little. Dan, don't pressure me. I feel warning bells telling me I need to be objective if I want to be helpful. I can't take a step closer and be objective." She averted her head as she placed the rubbing lotion on the bedside and quickly left the room.

Karen's thoughts were tumbling, disconnected masses as she stood with her forehead against the cool glass of the living room windows. Nighttime Denver was a blur of twinkling lights. The condominium was far enough from the center of city life to be swathed in darkness, but the view of streets below and beyond was of restless, constantly moving lights. The urgency of it all was discomforting and she was filled with longing for the quiet mountains.

Tina came to stand beside her. "Beautiful, isn't it? I love thinking of all those people, wondering about the exciting things they will be doing this evening."

Karen shuddered, "It's confusing, noisy. I wish I were in the mountains."

"You lived at a commune? What was it like?"

"Quiet, peace, and order, but good times and fun too."

"All good and no bad?"

She moved restlessly. "Pretty much so. The unhappy ones left soon, usually about the time an unpleasant task came up."

"Sounds typical of people everywhere. Were they all young?"

"For the most part." Karen wiggled her shoulders and wished she could leave without seeming rude.

"And they all meditate?" It was asked hesitantly but suddenly Karen felt childishly on the defensive.

"Look, Tina, I realize you don't see life as I do, but please don't expect me to come over to your way of thinking. I've tried it, and I don't like it. I don't like your view of God, pointing His finger at me and thundering, 'The wages of sin is death!' Up there I was taught the peaceful way to attain everything that fear has taught you. I don't intend to be changed."

"Have I said anything to you to make you think my view of God is like that?"

"Well, no." Karen was thinking carefully. "It's just that I know how I felt before I meditated. I had to be re-educated to know how to get around those feelings."

"Christmas tree lights."

"What?" Karen faltered.

"Karen, haven't you maybe just found a way to short-circuit your emotional response? You don't escape feelings or get around them. You must resolve them with God's help or you end up as nonfunctioning as an old-fashioned string of Christmas tree lights."

"What a wonderful sermon idea."

"You don't measure your relationship to God by how you feel. Truth is more concrete than that, and emotions can be warped."

"And you think you have truth; therefore my life has no value. You are judging." Feeling as if she had gone too far to stop now, Karen let the impulsive words continue. "I know what you are thinking about me. It's in your eyes. You are deciding that I'm the scum of the earth. Nice girls don't run away. Nice girls don't allow men to pick them up, marry them, and then discard that man like an old pair of jeans. But you don't know all that goes on inside of me. How can you really judge me? Shall I just give up on myself because you've decided there's nothing good about me?'' She turned on her heel and hurried down the hall.

"Karen," Irish called. She hesitated in the doorway of his darkened room. "I won't stand for your being rude to Tina." She couldn't miss the sarcasm in his voice. "Aren't you forgetting your own self-proclaimed role of bearer of peace and serenity?"

Turning one last glance at Tina, Karen asked through her teeth, "Does your thundering God have a red beard too?"

Chapter 6

Karen opened the door. The short, bald man with cold eyes said, "I'm Markham, this is Mr. Norris. Is Mr. St Clair at home?" She opened the door wider and Mr. Norris leered at her.

"I like the way he decorates his apartment," he said, winking at her. Silently Karen pressed against the wall and let them pass.

Later she carried coffee and cookies to the living room and unexpectedly Irish's eyes thanked her. As she worked in the kitchen she could hear the hard, cold voice of Markham and the overly jovial exclamation marks interjected by Mr. Norris.

She didn't hear enough of the conversation for the occasional words to have any significance; but the phrases "deeds of trust" and "security clauses" punctuated by "bank check" and "negotiated contracts" left her with a vague uneasiness.

Finally Irish walked with the men to the front door and Karen went after the coffee cups. When Irish returned to the living room it was to pace between the leather pouf and the windows. The frown on his face plummeted Karen back to those early months of their marriage when the reality of his new law practice was an empty office and secondhand furniture.

She was realizing that during the two years of their marriage, she had seen more of the frowns, increasingly more, than she ever saw of the happy-go-lucky person she had married. Now she realized the thunder-cloud expressions had become a way of life, something she had grown to expect. But to be honest, she needed to remind herself that she hadn't been the model of patience and comfort to him. She shrugged impatiently and sopped up a splash of coffee with a paper napkin.

It's karma, she acknowledged. *I hate to have to admit it, but I could have changed it all. If I'd been meditating then, he would have been a successful lawyer by now.* She stopped in the middle of her mopping job and looked around. This condominium and the furniture, surely they spelled success. The unanswered questions were bigger than ever.

Irish chuckled and she turned to look at him. There was a sheepish expression in his eyes as he caught her glance. "I was thinking of the time, right after we married, when you had my boss over for dinner."

"It was terrible."

"You were too young, didn't really know how to cook. I shouldn't have let you do it."

"I insisted. But how awful! Too much salt in the potatoes. I was so nervous it didn't occur to me to taste before I added salt the second time. And the soufflé—it ran all over the table as soon as I took the aluminum foil off."

Irish laughed with her. "The expression on his face."

"Oh, it was so awful and you kept saying, 'Never mind. I liked it.' But you drank a gallon of water after he left."

Irish's face lost its grin, but the tenderness in his eyes made her catch her breath. Fearful of his touch, she wanted to run, but she hung motionless.

Abruptly he turned away and then she could breathe again, breathe and wonder what foolishness to drag up that moment.

When he spoke again his voice was casual. "Karen," he was standing by the window asking, "how did that pair grab you?"

"Those men? I couldn't understand a thing they said, but the vibrations were all wrong."

Irish snorted and turned from the window. "That isn't what I meant. I don't have much confidence in vibrations, but I just want to know the overall impression they made on you."

"You're pretty troubled about something," she said slowly. She carried the wet napkins to the kitchen and returned to flop in the middle of the pouf.

"Just watching you makes my back hurt," he grinned down at her and prodded her foot with his own.

"But the pain won't last forever?"

"I hope not. Most of the pain is gone but the leg is still numb. I'm supposed to return for more X rays in a few days."

His expression sobered, "About Markham and Norris. They're my clients and I have no concrete reason to distrust them, but I keep feeling our working relationship is all wrong. Something just doesn't add up. Karen, what's right and wrong? I get the impression I'm working in a gray field where nothing is clear-cut and believable."

Karen shook her head slowly, "Can any human really know what's right or wrong? That's something too big for us to handle all on our own." She took a deep breath. "Irish, if you'd meditate, those problems would all be handled for you. When you are deeply into meditation, you automatically make the right choices."

"You aren't serious!" he exclaimed. "You don't really believe that. Karen, I don't understand much about God, but I'm sure I can't believe He'd give us a mind and the ability to think and then tell us to blot out our power to reason and choose."

The front door clicked and Irish turned. "Tina, come here. We're getting into something that I think is theological and neither of us knows where we're going."

With packages in her arms, Tina stood in the doorway and looked from one to the other. Her eyes were startled and there was almost a frown on her face. Karen pondered the expression and decided to Tina it suddenly looked as if she were the outsider, not Karen.

"She believes," Irish jerked his head toward Karen, "that meditation produces a deep knowledge of right."

"No, no, I didn't say that. I said deep meditation automatically makes you choose what is right."

"Without the necessity of thinking about it?" Tina asked.

"Well, no, you're to choose the thing that will bring happiness. That's how you judge rightness."

Tina lowered her bundles to the floor and tugged at her gloves, "Brr, it's cold out there. We're going to have one of those wet spring snowstorms."

Karen watched her place her coat across a chair. She was doing it slowly and deliberately as if she were stalling for time. "I can't accept that, Karen. God has given us reasoning ability. Surely He won't override that gift. He gives us intelligence and expects us to use it to question the right or wrong of the situations we face. We don't just judge them by our emotions."

"But you can't depend upon intelligence," Karen cried. "Life is full of choices. There's always a chance you'll be faced with a choice to make and you won't have any way of knowing the outcome."

"Karen," Tina's eyes were deeply troubled now and they filled Karen with an undefinable uneasiness, "choices aren't made on the basis of their outcome. They must be made only on the basis of what is truly right."

Karen was shaking her head, "But sometimes I don't know what is right. Tina, you've put me back out on the limb. How can I have peace and serenity if I must be faced with making choices like that?"

Looking genuinely concerned that Karen understand what she was saying, Tina explained, "Karen, we possess the key to right or wrong choices. That's built into us by God. The point of breakdown comes at the time of wrong choices."

"You mean I can no longer make right moral choices when I choose to make wrong ones?"

"Precisely." Tina nodded encouragement at Karen's question. "If making the right moral choices is important to you, you must consistently make them or the system fails."

"How do you know when it fails?" Irish asked.

"It failed in the beginning, at that time of the first choice. Adam and Eve." Karen noted Irish's startled expression. Tina continued. "That's the whole story of God's dealing with man. Man sinned and it got so bad, man couldn't even recognize his perversion. That's when God gave His law as a standard of right and wrong."

"Oh, and that automatically corrected everything?" Irish's voice was bitter and cynical.

"No," Tina answered thoughtfully. "I don't think you're interested enough to follow the whole story. If you were, you could read the whole right-wrong struggle in the Old Testament."

Irish protested, "You're leaving me dangling. Is there any solution?" Tina looked at Irish, and Karen saw her questioning look change to surprise and then triumph.

"Yes, the solution God planned all along. Through Jesus Christ He provided the moral basis, which is the only true way to know the difference between right and wrong. Acceptance of Christ as God's Messiah is the starting point.

"The relationship that results will provide a built-in

moral guide that will help you choose right. The guide is the Holy Spirit. But, Karen," she faced her, "never will He make the choice for you, or force you to choose it."

Later Karen was still pondering the conversation as she prepared dinner. All that Tina had said filled her with an uneasy sensation of walking on a very narrow fence. Karen dumped potatoes and carrots into the sink and reached for the peeler. At the commune, surrounded by those who believed as she did, everything had seemed so simple and believable. Moodily she stared at the potatoes. "I'm not meditating enough, reading enough. How long will it take to get over being confused by these other ideas?" She wished Lenny or Mark were here to explain it all to Irish and Tina and to tell her again.

The phone rang. Karen called, "Tina, please, I'm up to my elbows in potatoes."

Tina turned from the phone and placing her hand over the receiver, asked, "Dan, a Jeff Evin wants to call on you this evening. Will you see him?"

Coming to the doorway, Irish sighed and rubbed his hand across his face. "I suppose so. Have to get back in the saddle some time soon."

Karen finished peeling the potatoes and wiped her hands. "Saddle? Jeff is a lawyer. Why must you give him legal advice?"

"It's happened since you left," he said. "Jeff's suing his ex-wife."

"His ex-wife. I didn't know they were divorced. Whatever for?"

Karen couldn't miss the bitterness in his voice. "Sadie Evin took it upon herself to get rid of Jeff's child. It's an unprecedented case, but wild as it seems, I'm one hundred percent for it. It's about time someone thinks about the other two individuals involved."

Although Karen was beginning to guess, she whispered, "I don't think I understand."

"While they were still married, she had an abortion without consulting Jeff." His voice was gruff with emotion. "The feminist movement with their demand for rights has warped the thinking of much of society. You might say Jeff and I will put our time and money on the line for a case that's been lost ever since the right for abortion has been upheld. At least we'll be making the public sit up and question the validity of a woman's right to destroy life because it pleases her whim. That baby and that cheated father have rights too. Jeff wanted that baby. We both deeply feel there has been a wrongful death and intend to fight it from that position."

Out of the silence, during which she busily stuffed potato peelings down the garbage disposal, she couldn't help saying, "I didn't think you were all that interested in babies."

"That isn't the point," he paced the kitchen. "I love children and I think they should be a result of wanting and planning. Obviously a young lawyer isn't in the position to have a child; but, if the child's there, no decent, self-respecting person would deny birth simply because it doesn't happen to be convenient at the time. 'Abortion tears up the moral fiber of life.' That's a quote from someone else, but there's no other way to look at it. And if the mothers don't care, then the fathers must." Irish walked out of the kitchen.

Karen watched the cafe doors slowly swing back into position and realized how little she really knew Irish.

Tina came back into the kitchen. "What's the matter, Karen, are you ill? You're kind of pale."

"No, not really," she said pressing her hand against her stomach. "Just hungry, I suppose." She squared her shoulders and turned to the refrigerator.

"Karen, close the refrigerator. You've been staring at that tomato for five minutes," Tina said. "Shall I introduce you two? Mr. Tomato, this is Miss Karen. I mean, Mrs. Karen."

Karen looked at her laughing face, thinking, *"That's the problem. I'm Mrs. Karen and I didn't know how Irish felt. Oh, I wish . . . but then, it's too late for wishing.*

"We've met," she said slowly, "but my problem is, what do you do with one tomato and no lettuce?"

Two days later Karen stood beside the window and watched the snow fall. The fat, lazy flakes drifted past the window and out of sight. She guessed they would melt before they touched the ground. The roofs, trees, and the streets below were wet but not snow-covered.

The front door clicked and she turned. It would be Tina and Irish back from the hospital. He looked tired and his leg dragged more than usual.

"The X rays?"

"Don't know. The doctor will call later." He tossed a set of keys and a credit card to her. "There's a beat-up old Volkswagen parked downstairs. "It's a dirty, faded blue. Sorry I couldn't provide anything more colorful, but there wasn't a pink one on the lot." Momentarily his eyes twinkled. "It's to replace the car I wrecked," he explained. "It isn't much, but at least you'll have wheels to get you to the grocery store."

"Your beard is wet." He dabbed at the red whiskers. "When are you going to shave it off?" Karen asked, only half teasing.

"Why? I thought it looked pretty good."

"You're like a little boy hiding in the bushes."

"And I feel as if you are hiding behind that hair," he countered. "I'll make a deal; I'll shave, you cut your hair." Karen headed for the kitchen. "I'll even buy you a new pair of blue jeans," he called after her. "In another week you'll be able to see daylight through those."

When she stepped into the kitchen, she was shaking with anger. Unexplainable, irrational anger. More and more, she realized bleakly, Irish was making her carefully guarded peace slip. She knew now she must meditate more often.

Tina was standing at the sink painstakingly washing vegetables. "Hey," Karen teased, "you aren't preparing them for surgery, only eating."

Tina smiled and continued her task. Karen watched the slender, calm hands patiently handling the vegetables as if they were really important. Her blonde head, with every tidy hair in its appointed place, bent over her task. Karen could see the gentle slope of cheek, edged with a little smile and she knew the smile was for her. Karen recognized herself as rough, impetuous, and uncontrolled in contrast. The meditating wasn't doing much for her inner serenity.

She took a deep, careful breath but the words burst out in an impatient rush. "How do you manage it? Always, no matter what he says or I say, you are as calm and cool as vanilla ice cream."

"Cool, calm!" Tina's face lifted toward Karen. She gave a bitter laugh. "Thanks for the compliment. I'm glad I appear that way to someone. I've just been hitting myself over the head with some of the cold, hard facts called failure or sin or whatever. I've always tried to be level-headed and in control of myself." She was silent for a moment and then in an almost inaudible voice confessed, "I don't know what makes an old maid go off the deep end. Maybe this is really a deep character fault, you know, this need to be important to someone. I'd rather think of it as a passionate desire to lose myself in service to others, but it doesn't seem to be turning out that way."

Karen felt the despair and couldn't stand it. Now it was her turn to comfort. "No, no, don't feel that way. Irish. Well, he affects people. He isn't mine; don't you understand? He isn't mine now and I'll never want him again." Karen was looking down, and, because she couldn't bear that backward step that would reveal Tina's face, she turned and left the room.

It was almost dinner time when the doctor called. Irish took the call in the kitchen while Karen and Tina worked.

When he replaced the receiver, Irish leaned against the wall and watched them work. Karen passed with a bowl of tossed salad. While Tina checked the steak he said, "The doctor is pleased with the X rays. Said there's no evidence of a bone chip. Most likely a damaged nerve accounts for the leg problem. I'm to continue with therapy at the hospital but he said I could dismiss you."

"Oh, no." Karen came through the swinging doors. "Don't let Tina go." Her face was troubled as she looked from one to the other. "Please, Tina, can't you stay longer?"

She turned to Irish. "Since the company's paying for her, it won't matter, will it?"

Tina closed the oven door and turned, "The steak is done."

"Your salary is paid through the end of the week," Irish said casually. "You'll stay until then?"

The steak was the most tasteless one he had ever eaten. Irish could see that the others weren't enjoying it either. As he sawed at the meat he realized he hadn't given much thought to life beyond his recovery time. Would Karen stay after Tina left? She probably didn't consider her mission accomplished. How would this affect his relationship with Tina?

Karen was pushing her meat around on her plate. "Well, boss," Tina asked cheerfully, "may I have tomorrow off? I have errands and would like to check on the state of my apartment."

"We can manage one day without you, I suppose." Irish pushed his plate away.

"I guess I could drive him to the hospital for therapy," Karen said slowly.

"You won't need to. There's no therapy scheduled for tomorrow and he's off medication."

"What'll I do if he falls or something?" Karen asked as she nervously crumpled her paper napkin.

"Hey, I'm eavesdropping." They both turned and looked at him. "I think I know how a polygamist feels." Tina blushed and Karen turned to look at her. Irish was watching Karen closely, seeing the growing comprehension in her eyes as she looked from him to Tina's blushes.

Karen dropped her head and muttered, "Anyone for dessert?"

The next morning, as Tina prepared to leave for the day, she stepped into Irish's room. "Dan," she called toward the bathroom door, "I'm leaving now. See you about four. Do you want me to shop for you?"

He came out of his bathroom and she gasped. "Like it?" he asked self-consciously touching his newly shaven face.

"I'd never recognize you in a crowd. It makes you look," she paused, "bony and defenseless. Even your red hair isn't as overpowering."

"Well, don't get the idea you can order me around just because I no longer look like a Viking."

She laughed as she shrugged her way into her coat. "I've got to go or I'll miss my hair appointment."

As he patted shaving lotion on his smarting chin, he remembered his statement to Karen only the day before. He glanced at the scissors on the dresser and toyed with the idea.

Curiously the thought of forcing her to conform to the pattern he had set was intriguing. This new Karen was a bit of a problem. Thinking back he couldn't remember her refusing his slightest suggestion during their time together. Would she still be the submissive wife? He picked up the scissors.

Karen was curled in her favorite spot, the rya rug in its patch of sunlight. She aimlessly fiddled with the strands of yarn, flattening them and then combing them upright with her fingers.

"Is that the new position for meditating?"

"No," she said without looking up. "I've about given up on that. There are too many distractions around here." From the doorway he could see her face was troubled. He recalled Tina's verdict of some deep problem causing her unhappiness.

In the silence Karen looked up. Her eyes widened. As she studied his face, he noticed the first stirring of life, of genuine recognition. It was a recognition that acknowledged remembered things. Her lips parted, she gulped and said, "I'd forgotten how familiar you are. Now I know why men grow beards. They are so defenseless without them. Is it possible for you to be hurt?"

"Didn't you know that?"

She shook her head, "Not fighting Irish." She noticed the scissors. Slowly she put her hands to the fly away mass of hair.

"Come on, it's your turn."

"No, I'm not ready."

"You want to strip me of my defenses, but you're not willing to come out in the open." He tried to laugh as he said it and was surprised to find how difficult the light touch was. "Come on."

She dropped her hands and studied his face. "You look as if you have a question mark in the middle of your forehead," he said. "What is it?"

"Just why," she said slowly.

"I don't know. A whim perhaps. Is it a risk worth taking?" She seemed to ponder it for a moment. He saw her lips tighten and then she nodded.

"Okay, get a newspaper and come over to the window. I can't sit that long so you'll need to stand."

He saw her shut her eyes and hold her breath as he reached for the first smoky, frizzed lock. He worked quickly, trying to be done with it all before the fatigue and pain came. "Hey, underneath it's dark and curly like it was before."

82

"Don't make it too short," she pleaded.

"Yes, you must be a little Jewish boy again." He snipped the last lock and tossed the scissors to the paper. As he brushed the hair from her shoulders he was surprised by their delicate boniness.

"You've lost weight." He touched the softness of her arm and felt the unexpected response of his pulse. Curiously he touched her cheek.

Tipping her head back, she stared up at him. Her eyes darkened. It was as if she were deliberately veiling her feelings. "Irish, you don't go back. I can never be a little Jewish boy again. You only move forward, on and on."

"No, sometimes it's impossible to go on until you've first gone back. All the unsettled things must be settled."

She frowned and chewed at her lip. He noticed its soft fullness. Her eyes were looking beyond him, unaware of him. Irish touched her arm again but still she seemed remote, beyond his touch. Impatiently he moved. Grasping her arms, he bent his head to reach for the familiar lips. Quickly she pushed and spun out of his arms. From across the room she stared at him, her trembling hands reaching for her face.

"Isn't that a little dramatic?" he asked sarcastically. "The scissors are down there. I wasn't trying to stab you."

For a moment her eyes searched his face. Then, turning, she dashed down the hall. In a second, with shawl and canvas bag, she rushed out the front door.

"Lesson number one," he muttered, looking down at the snipped locks. "If you want to know how to feel like a worm, just try kissing your wife."

Karen found the faded blue Volkswagen. The keys Irish had given her unlocked the door. She was still trembling as she slid behind the wheel and tried to concentrate on quieting her tumbling emotions.

That lightly brushing kiss had been a revelation, a double one, she decided. Like a yanked plug, it had tumbled in all the old emotions including the yearning, aching love for Irish that she had supposed was gone. In addition it surfaced the nightmare of guilt and shame she couldn't seem to escape.

Again she reminded herself, "The past is dead." She winced at the word and stoically continued, "The past is gone and is to be forgotten. Only the future exists. Only the future will eradicate the past. Bad karma, horrible, horrible karma; you'll twist me and push me down." She sternly resisted the sobs that she knew would tear her apart, but her eyes were burning dry as she leaned wearily against the steering wheel and stared into space.

The thought of going back to that apartment to face Tina and Irish, and of having to practice the serenity and peace made her clasp her hands to her aching middle. "I will," she muttered. "I will and I'll succeed. I've got to do that much for him. Oh, I wish I could meditate now! I have a terrible feeling I'm going to get myself into deep trouble unless I manage it."

Again she drooped against the steering wheel and tried to compose herself. As a measure of quiet began to creep over her, she tried to reach for the tranquillity of meditation. But the final step that would take her beyond herself was impossible. She felt her palms damping with perspiration. Irritably she rubbed them against her jeans.

Unexpectedly, for the first time since she had returned to Denver, there was that sensation. Her eyes popped open and hastily she turned, studying the cluster of parked cars surrounding her. With her heightened sensitivity she knew again that feeling of being observed. The parking lot was empty, the cars devoid of life.

Now she identified the sensation as a moment of intense awareness, totally in contrast to the moment of nothingness that she had sought in meditation. Slowly the feeling slipped away from her, leaving her alone and lonely.

The car was parked in shadows that the spring sun couldn't reach and warm, and she found herself shivering.

"I guess I might as well try this thing," she muttered. "Irish said it was for grocery shopping, so Safeway, here we come."

The simple task of pushing the cart up and down the aisles was soothing. She took her time, slowly loading her cart.

"Karen, Doll! How good to see you!" She recognized Freddie's voice one moment before she was engulfed by steely arms and Chanel No. 5. Freddie propelled Karen toward the check-out stand. Karen surrendered her trip to the delicatessen and tried to concentrate on the office gossip. As she listened she berated herself for forgetting this store was only two blocks from Freddie's apartment. She stared up at the liberal display of red lipstick and oversized teeth and thought, *Imagine, I once hung on every syllable this woman uttered.* She shuddered.

Karen was swooped out the door and into the Cadillac parked close to the Volkswagen. Freddie settled Karen in the front seat. "Darling, you haven't said a word. Let me look at you. You were so pale and half out of your mind when you left. You don't look much better now. That haircut! You must try the new longer look. I know you'd be sweet in it."

Karen groped for the window. "Air? You really do look all in. Karen, surely you've forgotten that unfortunate incident." A brief flicker—was it contempt? "You must come back. You know I wouldn't have worried myself about you in the first place if it weren't for that wonderful talent. Fantastic imagination. I'd guess from the looks of you that you haven't even given a thought to designing lately. The rumor was that you were in a mental hospital."

"Commune," Karen almost shouted.

"Wonderful. I'm sure it did you a world of good. There's no sense letting little things upset you." She paused to giggle at her own humor. "Karen, we career women must be single-minded. We mustn't let anything or anyone drag us down. Now if you've fully recovered from that little incident, please come back to old Freddie."

Karen pushed the door open. "I'll let you know," she said weakly.

There was a flicker of concern in Freddie's hard eyes. "Dear me, you really don't look too well. I've heard things like that can unbalance a woman. I'd have guessed you to be stronger than that."

With Freddie's words echoing in her thoughts, Karen drove aimlessly. The afternoon shadows were long before she felt calm enough to face Irish and Tina.

After Karen's abrupt departure, Irish paced the living room. His thoughts were fragmented and emotional, and he was aware of being more lonely than he could ever remember except for those first months after Karen had left.

When Tina entered the apartment, he exclaimed, "Back so soon? I guessed it was Karen returning."

"It's almost four o'clock. Where is she?" Tina dropped her jacket on the leather couch. She seemed tired, he noticed.

"She tore out of here several hours ago. I don't know where she went." He quickly shifted his attention away from Karen's sudden departure. "Your hair looks nice and you smell like violets today. Was your apartment intact?"

"Yes." She was studying his face.

"What is it?"

"I was just thinking how much I'll miss this, even Karen. Oh, Dan, it's all such a mixed-up affair. If you must know, I had to get away and just cry. I never intended to get this involved in a situation that really shouldn't have included me." Her lips trembled and he reached for her hand. "Please, it isn't all self-pity; part of it's frustration. Karen yanks at my heart. I keep feeling as if I'd like to shake her back to reality."

86

"You can see how hopeless it all is."

"Yes, maybe, but what will become of her? Has she talked about her future?" Irish shook his head. In the silence the clock struck and the refrigerator hummed.

"You know," Tina murmured, "this is silly, but I've never thought about your really being hurt by all this until this morning when I saw you'd shaved off your beard. You seem so—"

"Vulnerable?"

She nodded and murmured, "Perhaps I've done you a disservice by being here." She bowed her head and he could see the tears on her face. Out of the ache Karen had started, he reached for her. He wanted to wrap his arms around Tina, to comfort her. But he also wanted to stop the aloneness that he felt by being close to someone.

The tearing grocery sack and bumping cans made them look up. There was Karen, holding the torn sack by one corner and staring at them. From the doorway she looked from one to the other and on the frozen whiteness of her face there was finally understanding and acceptance. She released the sack, turned slowly, and walked down the hall. They heard the front door close softly.

Tina started after her and Irish took her arm. "Don't," he said quietly. "Anything would be wrong now."

"I'll leave," she said. He nodded.

As she picked up her jacket, Irish said, "Give me your telephone number. I must have it."

Chapter 7

The Volkswagen was into the foothills before Karen thought to look at the gas gauge. She discovered it was almost touching the empty mark. Feeling as if she were in a dream, she coasted into the service station.

The attendant filled the tank and returned the credit card to her. "Where you headed?" he asked cheerfully.

"Well, I don't know. Where does this road go?"

He looked startled, "You lost?" She shook her head and he added. "It's 285. This is Morrison, you know, by Red Rocks amphitheater. Stay on it and you wind through a bunch of little mountain towns. You'll hit Fairplay on the other side of South Park. Look, wanta map?"

She nodded and followed him into the station. As he rummaged through the pile of maps she looked around. On impulse she asked, "May I charge things other than gasoline on the card?"

"Sure, whatever." There was a fuzzy, plaid car robe in a plastic case. She picked it up and reached for crackers and candy bars.

After she got back into the car, she drove beyond the cluster of houses and parked on the shoulder of the road. Taking a deep, shaky breath, she forced herself to exhale slowly. Her hands were still clutching the steering wheel, and she deliberately concentrated on relaxing them.

"Well, Karen," she reminded herself, "you did it again. You cut when the going got rough."

She reviewed the pattern that marked her life. When she met Irish, she had been running away from her father. Twice now it had been from Irish that she ran.

She thought of the past weeks and her resolve to create peace and happiness. "It'll never work. All my high resolves are more worthless than play money." For a moment she tried to honestly face that word that described it all. Failure. "I just can't do it. I've tried. This time I've slammed the door completely. I'll never go back." Bleakly she faced the alternative. "How far must I run to forget forever? Is there really such a thing as escaping your past when you can't change it or even make it right?" For a weak moment she squeezed her eyes shut, and then she straightened and reached for the canvas bag. There was a hundred dollars left of the money Irish had given her. And there was the credit card. She picked up the map and with one finger traced 285.

Her finger hesitated. She could go back to the commune. In considering it, now she was finally able to admit it had been losing its attraction long before she had returned to Denver. "I just outgrew the place."

Highway 285 went through the mountains and on to the plains. Her hand wavered on the thin red line. The car and the credit card were Irish's and he was no longer a part of her life. She winced. For some reason that fact brought more pain now than it ever had before.

She tried to understand her feelings. "It's just," she scornfully reminded herself, "that you've finally realized someone else wants him. A someone who's capable of making him happy."

She started the car. There was a tap on the window. "Hey, can I ride?" The boy looked about thirteen. "Oh, sorry, I thought you were a guy."

"Where are you going?" she asked. He gulped and shrugged his shoulders. She flipped the door handle. "Get in. So you're running away too?"

Dropping his bundle on the back seat, he shot a look at her. "You mean you are? I didn't think grown-up ladies ran away."

She felt her lips twist in a humorless grin. "I guess I'm not all that grown-up. Does twenty-four seem old to you?" He nodded. "So, now I'm helping a kid run away from home."

"Naw," he protested, "I'm not all that young. I just look that way."

"Because of the sheltered life you've lived?" She had noticed the dark bruise under one eye.

"Aw, my old man and me had a fight. He'll never listen and he's always right."

"So, what's the exception? All fathers are like that."

"Yeah, but they don't have to slug you just because of it."

"A smack, is that reason enough to run away?"

"It wasn't that so much," he said slowly. "It's the whole pile. Sooner or later it had to happen."

"I know. You can only take so much and the only way you can get even is by splitting."

"That's what it was with you?"

She could smile gently now. "No, for once. I just wasn't needed anymore. I guess my job was finished. No, to be honest, my job wasn't even started. It failed before it got off the ground, just like a paper airplane that's been folded all wrong. But what'll you do? You're too young to work. You know, you could end up in jail and the first thing they'd do is get your parents."

They were starting to climb. Karen shifted gears and concentrated on coaxing the laboring vehicle. At the top of the hill, the engine coughed and died.

"Oh, no!" she cried. "Can you give a shove? If I can coast, maybe it'll start."

From behind her a horn tooted and a van slowed long enough for two bearded fellows to hop out. "Stay there, kid, and we'll give you a shove."

The engine coughed and resumed its reassuring chug. She waved her hand and guided the car back into traffic.

"This isn't a very good car, is it?" her companion asked with a troubled frown.

"It's better than nothing. It may get us there and it may not," she stated grimly. "Do you know anything about cars?" He shook his head and gingerly leaned against the door jamb.

"Have you changed your mind?"

"You mean about splitting? Naw."

"You could hop across the road and catch a ride back before they know you are gone." She could see he was considering. "Got any money? You have to eat."

He shook his head. After a silent minute, he reluctantly said, "Well, maybe I'd better. He'll beat me worse if the police catch me." She drove to the shoulder and braked.

"Thanks, lady. I hope things work out for you." He managed a grin as she drove away.

It was getting dark and she was still in the mountains. She put her fears into words. "At twenty dollars a night for a motel, that money is going to be gone before I know it." How long would it take to reach California and find a job?

She was approaching a small town. On impulse she turned off the highway onto a winding dirt road. Her guess was correct. Within a short distance the road bumped to a finish beside an abandoned mine shaft.

Driving carefully around the fallen timbers that marked the entrance to the shaft, she eased the Volkswagen into a grove of aspen. When she turned off the engine, silence descended like a weighted curtain. Getting out of the car she moved around, trying to work the cramps out of her stiff legs.

The road had climbed from the highway, and below her

she could see the little mountain town settling down for the night. Smoke curled lazily and lights blinked. There was a faint toot of an auto horn and a muffled shout.

Civilization, she decided, feeling lonely, was a pretty nice thing after all. In the abandoned mining camp, the only neighborly sounds were the chirping of birds and the noisy protest of small scurrying animals.

A breeze made the timbers on the old mine shaft creak. "Is there anything more dead than the useless and forgotten?" she muttered as she picked up a pinecone and heaved it at the silvered boards.

She shivered in the cool mountain breeze and reached for the crocheted shawl. Something bumped against the floor boards of the Volkswagen and she discovered an apple. It reminded her of the splitting grocery sack and, against her will, she found herself reviewing that scene in the living room.

Her Irish with his long arms wound around that woman. *But, no, he isn't my Irish,* she sternly reminded herself. She had told Tina that never again did she want to be Irish's wife.

She jumped off the fender of the car and reached inside for the crackers and candy. "Dinner time," she said briskly, "and then it's night time. It'll be a long road tomorrow." An inquisitive squirrel came to watch her eat the apple and crackers.

At noon the next day, the car developed a desire to inch toward the right. She stopped on the shoulder and watched the right fender settle closer to the ground. She muttered, "I hope there's a spare." There wasn't and she slowly rolled toward town. A Cadillac shot past honking. A pickup stopped ahead of her and the gray-haired man in bibbed overalls shook his head over her woman ways.

"No spare?" He bent his head to examine it and shifted the straw he was chewing to the other side of his mouth. "Ruint anyway. Might as well keep going."

The garage didn't accept credit cards and Karen parted with a large portion of her money.

Back on the road she passed a drive-in and realized she was shaking with hunger. As she slowly ate the hamburger and fries, she felt as if she were emerging from a cocoon. She became aware of people and sun and wind and decisions that must be made.

Finishing the French fries, she slurped up the last of the milkshake and reached for the map. As she opened the map against the steering wheel, she wondered how long the money would last. Her finger followed 285. This little town was Poncha Springs. Soon she would be out of the mountains and it would be clear sailing until South Fork.

She patted the dashboard. "Dear little car, you aren't much of a mountain climber, but this afternoon you'll do your stuff across the flatlands."

Soberly she faced the fact it would take another day to get to Utah. How long would it take to cross Utah and Nevada? She regretted the dollar and a half spent for lunch. "Dinner will be out of a can."

It was late afternoon when she reached Alamosa. At the supermarket she spent a dollar for a can of stew and a can opener. Reluctantly she added fifty cents and bought a box of crackers.

It was almost dark when she reached South Fork and found a dirt road winding back into the mountains. She followed it and backed the car among the trees before getting out.

The wind was rising. It lashed the tops of the Douglas fir, filling the air with the sound of their protest. She snuggled deeper into the shawl and wished she could see the lights of South Fork. Twilight abruptly became darkness, deep and empty, except for the mournful communication between trees and wind.

Getting back into the car she clasped the can opener with cold-stiffened fingers and pried open the can of stew.

She was shivering as she forced herself to eat the congealed gravy and potatoes, to chew the tough, tasteless meat. She was almost numb with cold when she finally crawled into the rear seat and wrapped the fuzzy robe around herself. Gradually she relaxed and became drowsy.

The wind had lost its fury and she concentrated on the gentle music it created in the tops of the trees. How much she loved the mountains with their stately quietness and impersonal serenity. But how much better to be in the mountains with friends. Alone in the stillness it all was overwhelming.

During the night a piercing cry interrupted her dreams. Only as she shoved aside the folds of the robe did she realize where she was. She lay wide-eyed and tense, fighting not only the loneliness, but straining to understand the awakening moment that had sent her rebounding back in memory.

Irish had said that sometimes it is impossible to go on until you first go back. But he was wrong. He must be. The past had to be forgotten.

She had tried to forget and had attempted to make a new life. Was it really working? She thought of the process of escape and renewal she had gone through.

Walking out on Irish that first time was the only way possible. How deeply she recognized that flight had been a desperate act of self-preservation. Her hands trembled as she pulled the robe around her cold shoulders.

And where do you go when you run away? To the far ends of whatever you have been. To the opposite of it all. To those who denied material success or even need. To those who had discovered the opposite of material was spiritual and had quickly taught her that healing of a wounded spirit was found in the denial of all that wounds.

At the mountain commune they had taught her that the focus of life must be contact with a kind, benevolent God. Through submersion in Him, she discovered she was no

longer required to fight or struggle, or even to be subjected
to the dilemma of understanding the differences between
right and wrong.

Thinking about Tina and Irish, she moved her shoulders
impatiently against the hard cushions and wanted again to
make them see how wrong was their view of a thundering
God who demanded right and punished wrong. Even comparing the differences between their beliefs and hers filled
her with bursting frustration. She burrowed down into the
robe and tried to quiet her thoughts.

In the still and wakeful time, the nagging questions
reappeared. Why, if God is all benevolence, was she unable
to forget the past and find the way to enter into the deep
form of meditation she had experienced in the very beginning? Why was it becoming more difficult to meditate and
to automatically do the good she was supposed to do?

She reminded herself that she had been told she must
believe she was doing good. Reaffirming the belief didn't
help. A deep core of uneasiness remained and she spent the
rest of the night tossing on her uncomfortable bed.

It took most of the next day to coax the Volkswagen over
Wolf Creek Pass.

After she finally resigned herself to the chugging twenty
miles an hour the car was able to maintain on the steep
grade, she discovered the scenery.

Great masses of snow still bordered the highway, but
the meadows were shrugging off their white burden of snow
and the dots of lakes were free from ice. Beside the road,
under the protecting curve of the banked snow, she could
see the yellow avalanche lilies with their petals dripping
melting snow.

It was a bright, clear day. High clouds scooted across the
sky, but the wind barely moved the tops of the trees. Time
after time Karen stopped the car to walk to the edge and
peer down into the deeply shadowed canyon. At one spot
she pulled off into a large parking area which overlooked

the plains to the east. Here the mountain range parted and allowed a seemingly endless view of mountains rolling into the hazy blue of the distant plains. The beauty of the scene made her long to share it with someone. As she returned to the Volkswagen, she found herself wondering why she and Irish hadn't taken time to explore Colorado during their two years together.

By the time she reached the summit, she had lost her desire to hurry and she almost enjoyed chugging the steep grade in low grear. Now thick clouds were tumbling over the mountains, moving swiftly, and an unmistakable cloud of gray was trailing behind them.

"Snow," Karen muttered with dismay. "A good, old, Colorado spring snowstorm." With the sunshine of the day, that meant warm roads would quickly turn to a skating rink, especially for Volkswagens. She shifted gears and tried to outrun the storm.

At Pagosa Springs, the roads were still clear, and, thinking of her flattening funds, she kept on going. As she left the town behind, snow descended in a thick cloud of flakes that hid all but the patch of black highway in front of her. She slowed as much as she dared and wished for an opportunity to turn around.

There was a graveled road angling off to her right. She pressed the brakes and as promptly released them. The car slithered and then slid onto the graveled shoulder. The wheels caught and held. With shaking hands she guided the car onto the road and cautiously inched along, still looking for enough room to maneuver the car around.

Ahead bright lights loomed through the snow. As the wind briefly parted the curtain of flakes, she caught a glimpse of a restaurant and service station.

She noticed her hands were still trembling as she carefully steered the car toward the pumps. A man dashed toward her. "Regular," she called waving the credit card at him.

He adjusted the nozzle and asked, "You're not lost, are you?"

"Well, I don't think so. Does this road go back to Pagosa Springs?"

"No, it only follows the creek up a ways. There's a few homes on up, but the road dead-ends in less than ten miles. Unless a person's headed up to a private cabin, there's no place to go. Simon's cabins aren't open until the middle of May."

"And the highway is getting slick," she said slowly.

"Lady, the highway's closed from Pagosa Springs on west."

Signing the credit slip, she gave it back to him. She was shivering now and she realized staying in the car tonight was out of the question.

The door to the restaurant swung open and a gust of warm, food-flavored air surrounded her. Dark bundled figures hurried away and she eased the car into a spot beside the door.

The bowl of soup made her feel better, but it didn't solve any problems.

Trying to make herself inconspicuous, she huddled in the booth until the woman behind the counter turned off the outside lights.

At the cash register, Karen asked, "Is there a hotel around?"

The woman rang up the fifty-cent charge and turned to look at her. "No, and the nearest is Pagosa Springs. Where are you going?"

"Utah."

"You won't make it tonight." She was silent for a moment as she studied Karen's shawl and short dark curls. "Homer," she called over her shoulder to the man who had filled Karen's gas tank, "do you suppose Letty could put up another one tonight?"

The man's eyes were kind. Karen watched the pleasant

wrinkles appear around them as he chewed a toothpick before answering. "I 'spect so. But you stay here until we've finished up. It's only a couple hundred yards, but in the snow and dark, you'd never find it."

"May I help?" She was given a broom.

While she was sweeping behind the display case that held candy bars and junk jewelry and supported the cash register, Karen noticed the white cardboard stuck in the corner of the front window. It was a "Help Wanted" sign and it planted an idea.

Later she discovered Homer was right about finding the house. When she stepped out into the swirling snow, she couldn't believe anything existed beyond the gas pumps and restaurant. Clutching the canvas bag, she followed Homer down the snowy path through the trees. She could just barely see the outline of the log house as they approached. Then there were shallow wooden steps and a porch where they stamped snow from their feet before entering a kitchen full of warmth and light.

Karen decided she was in an old folks' home. With arms akimbo, Letty, Homer's wife, stood beside the wood-burning cookstove and pointed them out. Gramps rocked close to the warmth coming from the oven and across the oilcloth-covered table, squared in the middle of the big room, sat Aunt Sarah. She nodded while her bright eyes looked from the dish of beans in her lap to Karen and Homer.

Letty took Karen to the tiny room opening off the kitchen and then began setting out cookies and milk.

When Karen was flat in the feather bed under the pile of quilts, she lay wide-eyed and stunned. Just like that she was warm and safe, and just as casually as if she had been expected. Their hospitality was a surprising gesture, something that she didn't know existed apart from the commune.

The next morning she made a disconcerting discovery.

Her appearance wasn't important. Standing in the middle of the kitchen, she watched Aunt Sarah and Letty work, and she thought about it.

At the commune she had stuck out like a sore thumb until she had undergone the metamorphosis that had made her one of them. Again, in Denver, her differences had caused uneasiness in everyone. She thought of the woman at the bus stop, Marge, the nurses and doctors at the hospital, even Freddie.

Irish had been impatient with her appearance. Had he cut her hair in an effort to restore her to the image of sameness?

But here she immediately sensed acceptance and it went beyond the similarity between Gramp's overalls and her jeans, Aunt Sarah's crocheted shawl and her own. These people seemed to look beyond the outside appearance. Even as Karen was intrigued by their acceptance, she was uneasily aware of being stripped of the line of defense her differences had created.

After bacon, cut thick as ham and fried crisp, eggs, and creamy oatmeal, Karen stepped onto the porch. The sun blinded her with brightness, but the snow had made mounds of everything in sight. Beyond the gas pumps her Volkswagen was an oversized snowball. Close to the house evergreens sagged in a tired-arm way beneath their load of snow, and beyond them where the road should have been there was only unbroken white.

From behind her Letty said, "There's no call to plow this road today. They can't hold school in a snow like this. It'll surely be tomorrow before the plow gets here."

"I don't suppose there'll be a customer at the restaurant today," Homer spoke cheerfully from behind her.

"No, but it'd be a good day to do some cleaning." Letty turned. "Let me get Aunt Sarah and Gramps settled and I'll follow you over."

"I'd love to help." They studied her a minute and satisfied, nodded in unison.

Karen scrubbed tables and chairs, then polished the knotty pine wainscot. While washing the front window she noticed the cardboard again. At lunch time she mulled over it. "That card," she addressed Letty, "you still looking for someone?"

Letty seemed to be seeing the exterior Karen for the first time. "It's not much of a job for a pretty little thing like you. It's frying hamburgers and maybe filling in at the gas pumps. Besides, there's no place to live around here except with us. The nearest town is Pagosa Springs. The cabins up the way don't open until spring 'cause of the trouble with frozen pipes."

Karen studied the sandwich in front of her. "But I think it would be the kind of a job I need right now. Would you rent that bedroom to me?"

She could tell Letty was looking beyond her face now and she watched her nod slowly. "Homer just wants a good, steady hand and if it gives him a chance to help someone else, he'd do it any day."

When Letty told Homer, the lines around his eyes crinkled, he chewed his toothpick and finally nodded. Karen felt as if she didn't have a secret to hide.

"Karen's going to stay," Letty told Rosemarie, the woman who had waited on Karen the night before. Her expression was guarded.

"Karen's going to stay," she told Gramps and Aunt Sarah that evening and the atmosphere felt like home.

Karen didn't think there were surprises left until after dinner when Homer reached behind him for a big leather-bound Bible.

She guessed her surprise didn't show. As simply as if she had always been a part of the group, Homer shoved the Bible in front of her, shuffled the pages with his calloused fingers, and, pointing to the spot, instructed: "Read this'n."

Karen's tongue stumbled over the unfamiliar King James while her thoughts were busy trying to absorb and

understand. "The Lord is my shepherd; I shall not want,"
she read, puzzled by the simple word picture. "He restoreth
my soul." Her head jerked up. Had they guessed? Kindly
eyes focused on her and gentle nods encouraged her.

Once again stretched flat in the feather bed under the
quilts, she moved her lips to the rhythm of the words. "The
Lord is my shepherd; I shall not want, . . . He restoreth my
soul."

The snow plows came. Karen served coffee and sandwiches and learned to operate the gas pump. The banks of
the creek overflowed and the snow disappeared.

It was time for the first pay check. Karen and Aunt
Sarah drove into Pagosa Springs, and, while Aunt Sarah
bought crochet thread and a length of percale for quilt
blocks, Karen fingered the Levi's and finally selected a
flowered cotton dress. It looked like Rosemarie's.

After they left the shop, they walked slowly down Main
Street. Karen discovered that was a ritual. "The middle of
May and as warm as you could ask for," Aunt Sarah said,
leaning on Karen's arm, "considering that snow two weeks
ago, that is."

Karen watched two percale swathed figures approach
and, after the introductions, she found Aunt Sarah was as
slow with her friends as she was with her arthritis. Karen
lingered nearby while Aunt Sarah stood in the middle of the
sidewalk and visited.

The store windows with their crowded displays invited
closer attention. Karen identified the miners' tools and
kerosene lamps mixed in with the more familiar shovels
and rakes. The bell on the door tinkled and Karen caught a
glimpse of saddles and smelled their leather. The next shop
was a drugstore. The sight of familiar cosmetics and
colognes in the store window was a link with the past that
seemed distorted in the present.

Aunt Sarah limped toward her and they continued
down the street.

Imagine Freddie and Chanel No. 5 in this setting. Or for that matter, imagine Irish mingling with the farmers and cowboys.

Aunt Sarah jostled her arm. "That's the church. Homer and Letty can't get away on account of the restaurant, but maybe me and you could come. You need young folks."

Now that the weather had cleared and warmed, Homer's cafe and gas station hosted a constant stream of fishermen. The candy bars were shoved aside in the display case to make room for fishing lures and jars of salmon eggs.

One evening when Karen came back to the house after an unusually busy day, she found the beehive of activity had spread. Even Gramps was busy spearing donuts out of bubbling fat. Aunt Sarah had put awa the quilt blocks and she was polishing the mirror over the sink. Letty was busy at the oven.

"This smells better than the restaurant at high noon. What's up?" Karen asked.

"Jonathan is coming," Aunt Sarah stated, rubbing vigoriously.

"And Amy," Letty beamed.

"That's Letty and Homer's boy and his little girl," Gramps explained. He popped a donut into his mouth.

"Now, Papa, that's enough. Remember what the doctor said."

"One extry man and a bitty girl can't eat all the food you've cooked up."

"You'll need my bed," Karen exclaimed with dismay. She took the donut Gramps forked to her.

"No, he don't sleep there. Prefers the couch in the front room. Amy's two and he brings the playpen for her."

Karen swallowed and had to ask. "Isn't his wife coming?"

Letty's face momentarily saddened and she said, "She died a year ago. Cancer. That's why Jonathan won't sleep in that room. That wedding ring quilt was made special for them. But he'll get over it all. He's still young."

The lamplight reflected off her spectacles as she turned to Karen. "He's a teacher in Denver. Got a good job."

Karen felt a prickle of warning and sighed deeply. She should be flattered, not irritated. She moved her shoulders restlessly and said, "Well, give me something to do."

She discovered Jonathan shared her feelings. While the grandparents tossed Amy and passed her to Gramps, Karen saw the dismay on Jonathan's face.

Like his tiny, bright-haired daughter, Jonathan was blonde and blue-eyed. The barely healed hurt was still visible on his face. She thought, *He's come to relax and get away from it all and what does he find but a baited trap.*

She cornered him in the pantry after dinner. "Cool it," she whispered. "I'm not a loose female with a hunting license."

The apprehension in his eyes faded and he laughed. "Thanks. I suppose it stuck out all over my face."

"I thought it looked like conditioned response." He nodded and shoved the cookie jar back into place. She continued, "I guess it's best to explain. I'm on the run and not about to get mixed up again." He looked confused and Karen was sorry she had said so much.

Jonathan and Amy stayed the weekend. On the first evening Karen discovered an interesting thing about Jonathan. When Homer reached for the Bible, Jonathan looked neither bored nor uneasy. He accepted the Book from his father and read as if he enjoyed it, not, as Karen had expected, as if he were humoring the old people.

The next day Homer sent her away from the restaurant early. "You've been putting in too many long hours. If you don't take time off, I'll have to pay you more. Besides," his expression was bland, "Jonathan could use a little company."

"You transparent old dear," Karen muttered as she walked back to the house. "Something tells me you are going to be disappointed."

Letty shoved them out the door. "Go take that baby down to Simon's pasture. The lambs are just gettin' cute."

They leaned over the split rail fence and watched Mr. Simon gently separate a lamb from a length of wild morning glory. Karen looked at his big, careful hands and listened to his soothing voice. She remembered the first verses she had read from Homer's Bible. "The Lord is my shepherd," she murmured.

Jonathan turned to face her as he leaned against the fence. The wind wafted the green grass fragrance of the pasture to them as he slowly quoted, "He shall feed his flock like a shepherd: he shall gather the lambs with his arm, and carry them in his bosom, and shall gently lead those that are with young."

Karen turned away. Touching her face, she wondered if her expression were as easily read as his. She forced a laugh and said, "It's a good thing we don't take literally all the Book says."

"How can you choose?" he asked. "I wouldn't know which part I could leave out. Instead, aren't those words there for us to prove in our own lives?"

Amy touched Karen's knee and Karen looked down into the flower-perfect face. She found herself squeezing her eyes shut and she moved carefully away from the groping baby hand.

Jonathan reached for his daughter and swung her up to the rail. Mr. Simon got to his feet. Lifting the lamb, he cuddled it in his big hands and held it out to Amy.

Karen stepped back to watch the lambs as they bounced around the pasture, tumbling in their eagerness, completely unafraid. Amy leaned out of Jonathan's arms and grasping a double handful of soft wool, she pulled the lamb's face against her own.

"Lambs and children," Karen murmured, "they're all unafraid." She watched a lamb suck Mr. Simon's finger. "I wish it were possible to draw a big, warm circle around young things, a hedge that would protect and keep them safe forever." The sun was gone and she shivered.

Chapter 8

Irish fingered the two paper-backed books in his lap. One was a New English Bible New Testament and the other was a book by C. S. Lewis. The latter was a book Tina had left for him to read, and the former an impulse purchase at the corner drugstore. Both, he discovered, were alien and irritating.

Getting out of the deep leather chair, he concentrated on flexing each pain-filled muscle. There were those that had been cut and torn during the accident and those which had lain idle much too long.

In the silence of the apartment, the clock gonged one deep note. It seemed the sound echoed from the walls and silent, empty spaces. He walked to the window and looked out over Denver. His skyline view of the rectangles and squares was almost hidden by the trees in full leaf.

It was now the middle of May. Two weeks had passed since both Tina and Karen had left. It had been two weeks of silence and inactivity; two weeks alone with the books and his thoughts.

Now he felt as if his mind were a conglomerate of ideas from C. S. Lewis. And there was the burning question St. Paul had posed. Although he had read little from the New

Testament, he couldn't seem to forget that one statement. In words that wouldn't be ignored, Paul admonished him to examine himself to see if he were in the faith. Even as he read Lewis, the statement of Paul kept popping up.

Lewis advised him to add up the facts, and, if the facts he knew indicated Christ was indeed God and His message truth, then he had better act upon the message. So well and good, he acknowledged, neatly filing away the idea as acted upon until he discovered another statement that was still teasing at his thoughts.

Lewis indicated that a view he called "liberal Christianity" felt free to ignore the difficult or unpleasant parts of the Bible. Irish had only given a passing thought to the idea until the rest of the statement burned its way into his mind with a stack of unanswered questions. Lewis said this kind of Christianity must be stagnant, for Christian growth could come only through acceptance of the difficult or repellent doctrines. And while the idea of Christian growth intrigued him, the two words "difficult" or "repellent" nagged.

Standing at the window made Irish's back ache. He turned and paced back and forth. It was Tina who had gotten him started on all this. How did she feel about it all? He wondered if some of the things in her life that interested him, as well as irritated him, were influenced by these ideas. It might account for the strengths and the stubbornness he sensed in her.

Realizing how lonely he was, he reached for the phone. "Oh, did I miss a therapy session?" she asked, recognizing his voice.

"No, I've been reading your book. What do you consider difficult or repellent doctrines?"

"It depends on your position," she said slowly. "The most elemental can be difficult to some."

"I've a steak in the freezer. Would you consider cooking it for me?" The silence was long and he realized all the implications of it. "Look, Tina, I am lonesome for you. But more than that, I need to talk. I promise, the next embrace will be your idea not mine." Silence. "Aren't we adult enough?"

"I'll be there in twenty minutes."

He was still pacing the floor when he heard her at the door. She hung her coat in the closet and came into the living room. There were dark smudges under her eyes and he thought she acted tired. "Hi, I'll start the steak."

The oven was preheating and the steak was on the rack. He watched her pull tomatoes and lettuce from the refrigerator. "There's French bread," he said. "I'll make croutons. Want garlic?"

He melted butter and diced bread. "Tina, this whole situation has me going in circles. Could we talk about it?"

"Dan," her forehead was puckered in an uneasy frown. "You need time to get straightened out in your thinking. I'm here to help."

"Funny, I'd have said the same thing about you."

"Then we both. Let's not talk about us for at least a month. Okay?" Unexpectedly he was relieved. He nodded and reached for the plates.

After dinner Irish pushed his coffee cup away and rested his elbows on the table. "Tina, for you, what were some of those difficult doctrines?"

She thought for a minute, "Do you mean in the beginning?"

"Yes, but even now."

"Let's take the beginning," she said slowly. "First was sin. It's a long way to go to be able to admit you're a sinner when you've spent all your life telling yourself how great you are. To bring up guilt and do something about it is the most difficult. And then there is the reality of Christ."

He frowned and she tried to explain. "See, with God you get the idea of remoteness and grandeur. This all seems a step away from anything to do with man. But with Jesus it is all different. It's grasping the fact that He was God as well as human. And then that He was willing to be subject to the Father's plan, just like any other human must be. That He was willing to be hurt, to be tempted, even to sit back and just take the rejection. I don't know about you, but this all makes me feel a greater sense of responsibility to Him."

"I don't see that."

"He said that what He could do, we can do also, and He wasn't just talking about miracles. He meant make a success of life in God's way."

Long after Tina left, Irish stood at the window overlooking Denver and mulled over the things she had said. He examined all that he knew about her and tried to fit it to the principles she had talked about. When he finally gave up, it was dark. The halo of light behind the distant mountains had faded too, and he returned to his chair.

Flipping on the lamp he settled himself in the recliner and picked up the New Testament. Without a doubt he'd never really know what made Tina what she was until he knew what was in her guidebook.

Without enthusiasm he thumbed through the Book. The first thing she had mentioned was sin. That was something that had been taken care of when he was a child. That act of baptism, that declaration of faith, was a past incident and he shook his head over Tina's emotional statement of something that was just fact.

Irish adjusted the recliner and thought the whole idea of religion was an uncomfortable thing to dwell on. He would give it all up in a moment if it weren't for Tina. Now he found himself comparing Tina and Karen.

"They're as different as it is possible for two people to be," he muttered. "Tina is steady, confident, and she seems to have a deep unshakeable serenity that Karen, regardless of all she's said about meditation, just doesn't possess."

Thinking about Karen unexpectedly released the flood

of painful memories again and that took him down the familiar aching pattern of bewilderment. What had gone wrong? What had taken away that Karen with her soft arms and tender kisses, the woman who had clung and adored?

He shoved aside emotions and admitted that Karen had disappeared long before she left him. During the last eighteen months of their time together, she had been changing. To be sure, the change was gradual, almost unnoticed, unless you compared the picture of the Karen he had married and the Karen who had walked out of his life without a word. Mentally he held them up. The one was happy, laughing, and full of life. The other was pale and silent, with shadowed blue eyes. That latter Karen had formed the habit of jumping when a door slammed, and to his disgust, seemed to cry in secret and at the most unexpected moments.

Irish struggled out of the chair and paced the floor in quick, hard steps. This was one night he wished he had stocked the liquor cabinet. He paused in front of the walnut cabinet and touched its smooth dark surface. *Status symbol*, he thought wryly; *just another symbol of another step up*. He swung the door open. There was a can of mixed salted nuts and he couldn't help grinning. "And nuts to status symbols," he muttered.

Somehow he felt better as he went back to the chair and picked up C. S. Lewis. With dogged determination he set himself to get through the book, although he had already discovered Lewis' terse statements cut clear to the bone, making him almost too wary to turn the page.

Karen was standing beside the table watching Aunt Sarah fit quilt blocks together. Letty picked up Amy and turned around. There was a puzzled expression on her face. "How come you never touch the young-un? Don't you like babies?"

Caught off guard, Karen stammered, "I, I just don't know much about them."

"Where were you raised that you never baby-sat?"

From across the room Jonathan spoke, "Mom, don't. Not everyone could possibly dote on your granddaughter the way you do."

Karen gave him a relieved smile. While she was grateful Jonathan had spared her the necessity of talking about her past, she couldn't help wondering how these people would react to the picture of the little girl that had been. There was the picture of the primly dressed little Karen with her governness; Karen in the sterile perfection of a home where fingerprints and running and shouting weren't allowed. Would they be sympathetic with that motherless, lonely child? Or would they, like her father, always find room to disapprove of her?

She shrugged off the thoughts impatiently, as she always did when she found herself unexpectedly trapped by the past. She was aware of Aunt Sarah's kindly gaze. Even Gramps' blue eyes were focused on her with an expression that made her heart feel as if it would burst.

She bent over the old man and pressed her lips against his tufty, white hair. "Jonathan has so many lovely people to belong to."

Karen was uneasily aware of the undercurrent of feeling in the room, and Letty's silence reminded her of the one fact that was always on her mind: Amy didn't have a mother.

Abruptly Letty hurried to the pantry and began carrying out butter and eggs and the big yellow mixing bowl. "Rosemarie says," her voice was crisp as she addressed Karen, "that you go on. She can handle it all today. Last week you worked for her on your day off." Now she faced her son. "Jonathan, why don't you and Karen drive up the way? It'd be a nice day to hike to the cabins."

"Want to go rummage around in a ghost town?" Jonathan caught his daughter on the run and carried her to the sink.

Over her protests he applied the soapy washcloth. "Going to spend the rest of your life with a dirty face?" Karen admired his easy way with the tiny, squirming figure even as she felt the familiar shrinking inside.

"Come on," Aunt Sarah coaxed, "we'll make you a nice lunch." She sliced bread and Karen reluctantly went to help her with the ham and cheese. As she wrapped cookies, Aunt Sarah reached across the table and patted her hand. Karen blinked at sudden tears.

Jonathan and Karen took Homer's old pickup to the end of the graveled road. Karen discovered the road ended on the bank of a swiftly running stream. Getting out of the vehicle, Jonathan pointed to the logs that crossed the stream in a haphazard fashion. "That was a bridge at one time. If you're nimble, we can cross it. Otherwise we'll wade."

"Ba-a-a!"

He glanced at her curly hair. "You look more like a black sheep than a mountain goat." Karen started for the bridge and he caught her arm. "Sorry," he murmured, "that wasn't meant to hurt. I think little black lambs are nice."

"But they're still black." Silently they crossed the stream and started up the ruined road. Underneath their feet the ground was still spongy while the bank above the road was alive with miniature waterfalls. "Oh, I love this mountain smell," Karen said, taking a deep breath.

From a distant place came the crash of water. "See how the rocks have almost covered the trail?" Jonathan pointed. "The heavy snows, sliding and melting, are responsible for that. This road goes up the hill about a mile to an abandoned mining camp."

"What are these flowers?"

"That's lupine, the first of the season. It's a little early for most of them, but in July this trail is lined with wild flowers. There's red Indian paintbrush, yellow dwarf sunflowers, mountain harebell and even some mariposa lilies."

The road dipped down and bordered the stream for a ways. "The runoff's begun," he murmured. "That means the high mountain snow is starting to melt."

"The water's muddy."

"Melting snow carries a lot of soil. It'll clear in a week or so."

The sun had warmed the trees and the air was scented with their pungent pine perfume. Along the creek the pines towered, allowing them to see only a strip of blue sky edged with clouds. When the road zigzagged up the mountainside again, the trees were left behind.

They were breathless from the climb when they reached the top. Rounding a knoll they found the abandoned ruins of the mining camp cupped in the hollow before them. As they wandered slowly through the town on the cindered strip that was yielding to the intrusion of grass and wild roses, Karen tried to visualize the ore-sprinkled hills and gray buildings busy with life. "It's certainly a dead looking place now," she said. "I can't imagine the lusty life these towns were supposed to have had."

They picked their way through the old buildings and peered down a mine shaft. Jonathan dropped a rock and it seemed forever before they heard it strike bottom. Karen poked through rusted cans and broken bottles. She tried to read the strips of yellowed paper that had been stuffed into cracks between the logs.

"Everything's so little. Can you see a family with a bunch of kids crammed into this little house? Or the saloon being big enough for the kind of rip-roaring gun fights that were supposed to have taken place in towns like this?"

"Karen, I think the gun fights were in the street."

They sat on crumbling logs and ate the sandwiches and cookies. In the mountain stillness bees tumbled in and out of the dandelions while crickets bravely resumed their concert. Jonathan's eyes were heavy-lidded and Karen smothered a yawn.

Out of the silence he said, "I've come to see if I may leave Amy while I go to summer school."

She looked at him out of the corner of her eye and wondered why he needed to explain. "You saw them. They'll never give up hope."

"Well, you are young and they want you to be happy."

"Want to tell me about it?"

Karen jumped, "Me?"

"I keep getting the impression you need a listening post, a something instead of a someone."

"That's a strange thing to say," she studied his sleepy face.

"This old man is pretty good at it—listening, that is," he broke a stick between his fingers. Abruptly he sat up. "Karen, are you a Christian? While Dad's been having devotions, I've been getting these strange impressions that mentally you are standing about six feet away from the rest of us. And every once in a while someone says something and you just about come unstrung. For instance, that remark today about Amy. What's wrong?"

She jumped to her feet and carefully said, "Jonathan, I just don't want to talk about it. Thanks for your offer, but—"

"Okay, sit down." They sat in silence for a long time. Finally, "Karen, you've seen the kind of people my parents are. They have the completely simple faith of children. They've never questioned God or His Word. Both were raised by people who believed in the Christian way, and what was good enough for their parents has been good enough for them. I guess that's a fine way to be, but not all of us are like that. I wasn't. I've questioned everything I've ever been told. I've had to satisfy my own mind, prove to my satisfaction that there is a God and that He's just as they say. It hasn't been easy and I wish I could save people the years of wandering around in a faithless intellectual maze that I've had, but I don't know how to go about it all. Karen, I know the search for God begins with need, but the end of it all still must be faith."

He was silent for a long time. She guessed from watching the bowed head and the white-knuckled hands pushed against his knees that his emotion ran much deeper than his easy, conversational tone indicated. "Unfortunately, my point of need came when my wife and I found out about the cancer. We did have one wonderful year to prove all He said. That, in the final analysis, was all anyone could ask for, just to prove Him true to His Word."

Karen couldn't help asking, "What did He say?"

"Things like, 'Come unto me, ye who are burdened and heavy laden, and I will give you rest.' 'My peace, not as the world giveth, give I you'; then 'Ye must be born again'; and 'Except ye become as little children. . . .' "

"I like that," she murmured caught by the tide of words, "born again, an all new start in life. Little children aren't really afraid of anything, are they? In the beginning, that is." She looked up at him and it was with a sense of crashing back to earth. Jonathan had only chosen the good parts, the comforting ones. There were the other ones. She could only watch him, wondering how long it would take him to move out of his unreal haze of sorrow and be able to face the harsh realities of life again.

"It's late, Jonathan," she reminded gently. "We'd better start back." She couldn't press through his sorrow and remind him he was doing that thing he had chided her for doing—picking and choosing from the black Book.

After dinner that evening, as Karen carried the last plate from the table, Homer said, "Karen, the Bible's on the desk; will you bring it?"

As Karen leaned over to pick up the heavy Book, it slipped from her hands. She scrambled and retrieved it

halfway to the floor. The open pages revealed a red underlined verse. She glanced at the heading. It was Jeremiah,
and she saw the words, "Can any hide himself in secret
places that I shall not see him? saith the Lord. Do not I fill
heaven and earth? saith the Lord." Abruptly she recalled
those experiences of feeling watched. She glanced at the
words again. If one were to believe this, well it could have
been God. But if that were so, why didn't the experience occur during meditation?

Still thinking she slowly returned to the table. She remembered those times hadn't proven fearful. There had
just been the sensation of not being alone. Was it possible
that God could be something different from what she had
always believed?

When Homer began to read out of the leather-bound
Book, Karen felt, almost against her will, that she was mentally moving away from the impact of the words. Suddenly
they penetrated, pushing in regardless of her unwillingness.
Homer read, "For my thoughts are not your thoughts,
neither are your ways my ways, saith the Lord. For as the
heavens are higher than the earth, so are my ways higher
than your ways, and my thoughts than your thoughts."

She pondered the accusation. That was contradictory to
what she had been taught. New words caught her.
" . . . but it shall accomplish that which I please . . . pros-
per in the thing whereto I sent it."

She jumped to her feet and backed away from the table.
"That says God's Word will do what He pleases, that it will
accomplish what He wants. It says God is inescapable."
Slowly she put her hand to her throat. In the silence she
heard the ticking clock and each tick struck her mind with
the cadence of the inevitable.

"I don't believe the way you do," she whispered. "Your
God is demanding and cruel. He crushes wrong—people.
That isn't correct. The idea of wrong is a fallacy. Guilt is a
mirage. Let me tell you, God is really good and there's no
wrong."

Their faces lost their startled expressions and became closed, unreadable. She realized the futility of saying more, but she couldn't help explaining. "You see, all I want out of life is to be free, and that means freedom to grow into being a complete person. That can never happen with your view of God and life."

The following morning Karen was at the restaurant early for the breakfast rush. Caught in the flurry of activity, she plopped platters of ham and eggs in front of the fishermen and reached for the coffee pot. "How's fishing?"

"Good, if you want to hike far enough away from the fished-out holes."

She moved away from them and began to clear dirty dishes from the tables.

Now the peak of the rush was over, and the air in the restaurant was slowly losing its aroma of ham and eggs and coffee. The cash register rang and the door creaked once more as Karen sponged tables and pushed salt and pepper back to their corner.

Her mind seemed to free itself from the mundane tasks and to step deeply into quietness. She recognized the prod to meditate and, as the door creaked for the last time, she slipped into the booth and closed her eyes. *Arms relax,* she ordered. The spiral of quietness began.

"Karen, are you ill?" Her eyes popped open. Jonathan was bending over her, his hand reaching for her forehead.

"No." Her irritation was in her voice. "I'm trying to meditate." She thought he looked as if a light bulb had been flipped on. A careful expression crept over his face. Amused, she watched as he slipped into the booth.

"This is what I wanted to say last night, but you all looked as if you'd slammed the door on me. Jonathan, you think you have something to help you cope with life, but let me tell you about meditating; it's better. You see, meditating puts you in tune with God, teaches you to surrender before Him until you actually merge with Him. There's quiet-

116

ness and serenity. After meditating you're so much more capable of coping with life."

"But I'm not having any problems. Is that all there is to it?"

"Isn't that everything? To be able to have peace and happiness as well as freedom from the pressures of life?"

"What's the idea behind it all?"

"Total serenity, total merging with God. The final goal is to get everyone in this world to meditate and then—only then will there be peace."

"Well, tell me how to do it."

She shook her head, "I can't. You'll have to take classes to get your mantra. That's the word you say over and over to help you meditate."

"What does it mean?"

"I don't know and don't ask me to repeat the word, because we're not allowed to tell."

"So you could be saying anything from life is beautiful to the most vile of words and you wouldn't know."

"Oh, Jonathan, you've got to believe they wouldn't teach you that."

"Is that all you do? Just go get a mantra?"

"Well, no. In the beginning you must be in the proper mood or state of mind. You go taking flowers, fruit, and a clean, white hanky. When you present your offering, you bow down."

His strange expression made Karen uneasy. "Do you know that is the way of Hindu worship—with the flowers, fruit and cloth? Isn't it possible you are worshipping a Hindu god?"

"But it's all the same God. What difference does it make?"

He leaned across the table and grasped her shoulder. Forcing her to look at him, he quietly commanded, "Karen, listen. What did they tell you about Jesus Christ?"

"That He was a great teacher like Buddha and some of the other great ones."

"Jesus told Philip that anyone who had seen Him had seen the Father. He said He was in the Father and the Father in Him. Does that sound like just a great teacher?"

"Maybe they don't know."

Jonathan shook his head. "God's Word says, and I'm quoting, 'Everyone who has listened to the Father and learned from him comes to me.' Karen, in John, the tenth chapter, Jesus says that anyone who climbs in over the fence is a thief and a robber. He said that to illustrate that He alone is the door to God. You've got to go through that door if you want to make it to God."

"I don't care. Right or wrong, I won't give up this wonderful peace."

"You would rather have an illusion of life, of truth, than the real thing?"

She jumped to her feet. "I told you last night, I don't like your God. Yours cuts you to pieces and mine brings peace and happiness."

"Yet you said He was the same." Jonathan shook his head and got to his feet.

Chapter 9

Pain awakened Irish. In the moment before he was fully conscious, he rolled and reached across the bed. The crisp, cold sheet under his groping hand made him realize he had been searching for Karen.

Getting out of bed he went to the bathroom for aspirin and water. Still confused and surprised by the revelation his groping hand had brought, he pulled on a robe and padded through the silent apartment. Moonlight streamed through the living room windows, and he skirted the dark shadows of furniture and walked to the window. The twinkling lights of Denver seemed to underscore his loneliness and he paced the room, waiting for the aspirin to dull the pain.

It had been a long time since he had unconsciously reached for Karen. He reminded himself that this new apartment was supposed to take care of those memories. Certainly the leather and chrome were far removed from the faded and lumpy furniture with which they had furnished their first apartment. But right now he was realizing the cold lights of Denver didn't help promote the cozy home feeling he wanted.

Karen. Where was she? The aspirin wasn't doing its job and he eased himself into the recliner.

Like a silent miniature figure doing vigilance, the dieffenbachia drooped beside the window. He pried himself out of the chair and went for a glass of water. Moving stiffly he bent and poured the water. "Sorry, old chap. I keep forgetting the water. Both of us could use a feminine touch around here."

He tried to concentrate on Tina, but his thoughts kept wandering back to Karen. Still puzzling over her, he again found his memory dragging up pictures of her, trying to understand what had happened. He took the glass to the kitchen.

Back in the chair, he tried to get comfortable and to think logically. "Admit it, old man, you're not going to have a hundred percent success with everything in life. Count Karen out as a failure and forget her. She's made her choice and therefore . . ." He paused.

The "therefore" made him feel like a lawyer again. How much, he wondered, of our image is mental? The cool, detached, and objective view of a successful lawyer was something he'd tried hard to maintain. Sometimes, like at three in the morning when his back hurt, the image slipped and became unimportant.

He quit trying to think and allowed his mind to wander. Soft, gentle Karen with her laughing lips. Tina and her sane and sensible approach to life. Dutifully he flipped on the lamp and reached for the New Testament.

Funny, Tina talked about God and the Bible with a passion, while to him it was a lifeless subject. Except for that one phrase. He reviewed it. "Examine yourselves: are you living the life of faith?" He moved restlessly and tried to remember the rest. It was something about putting yourself to the test. The whole thing seemed redundant, a rehashing of something that should be settled and forgotten.

C. S. Lewis declared that if a person had proven to his

own satisfaction Christianity was correct, the only logical conclusion to provable facts, then he had better go along with the whole idea. Surely that seemed to settle the whole affair.

Irish was aware of a nebulous loophole in his thinking that left him with a feeling of dissatisfaction. He pushed himself out of the chair and cautiously stretched. Perhaps he was shortchanging himself by not reading more of Lewis.

The dawn was a pink smear in the sky. As he went into the kitchen to make coffee, he reflected on the sense of un-finished business the night thoughts had left. Certainly Karen was unfinished business, but there was nothing he could do about that. And Tina? Tina was the most com-plete and logical subject he had thought about all night.

Two days later he dialed Tina's number. "Lady," he said when she answered, "I need a good, reliable chauffeur this weekend. What are your rates?"

He heard her suck in her breath. It had been over a week since he had seen her, long enough for him to find he was re-gretting that the therapy sessions had ended.

"Dan, what are you up to now?"

"I've heard from Markham. Bloomington is ready to make some pretty good motions toward a settlement and Markham wants me to wave a bank check under his nose. He insists on the personal touch. Tina, have you ever seen a redheaded farmer?"

"Not with a back brace. Would you really go that far?"

"It's starting to look as if I may have to. I'm pretty well committed to Markham's interests." Attempting to be cas-ual, he continued, "It might be a good idea for you to take a look at the place."

There was silence and he wondered if he had said too much. He chewed his lip and wished he could understand Tina's reluctance.

It was just after ten on Friday morning when Tina came

out of her apartment complex carrying an overnight bag
and a sack of apples. Irish got out of the station wagon to let
her in behind the wheel. "Sorry to make you drive," he
apologized, "but I still can't get across town without my
back complaining. I rented a station wagon so I can stretch
out when it becomes uncomfortable."

She nodded and said, "It's too bad your Mr. Markham
couldn't wait another week."

"I have a feeling he was interested in the psychological
impact of the limp and the back brace."

In silence they crossed Denver to the interstate. Out of
the heavy traffic, Tina increased her speed and relaxed.
"Are you continuing your exercises at home?" He nodded.
After more silence, Tina once again asked, "How's C. S.
Lewis coming? Are you enjoying the book?"

"I haven't read much, but I like the way he speaks:
straight from the shoulder without a lot of sentimental
double talk. It's got to be an unemotional and purely objective stance to interest me."

"You didn't read much." More silence. "Have you
heard from Karen?"

He moved impatiently, "No, and judging from last
time, I don't expect to. Tina, you keep bringing up Karen. I
would guess you're trying to uncover some terrible character flaw in me that will explain her leaving. Can't you
just accept the fact that we didn't hit it off together and
there's no solution to the problem except divorce. Karen
was a sweet little kid when I married her. She changed and
I suppose I changed too."

"Dan, I'm sorry. I'm not picking at you. It's just that I
am interested and I do feel terribly responsible for all this."

"Because I hugged you? Before that hug she'd guessed
how I felt. Also, before I left the hospital, she indicated she
hadn't come to stay."

Their talk wasn't accomplishing anything. By the time
they reached the dirt road that cut across the rolling hills to

the Bloomington ranch, he was aware that they were hedging around all of the important issues.

Tina's expression was becoming increasingly troubled and finally he said, "Look, let's find something else to talk about, something interesting like the weather."

"Dan, I'm sorry, but it's because there are things I just can't talk about now." She turned briefly from the wheel and touched his arm. Her expression was carefully controlled and she tried to smile. "I suppose it's the feeling that I mustn't say the important things, that you've got to discover them for yourself."

As the crow would fly, they were less than a mile and a half from the Bloomington ranch when Tina exclaimed, "Oh, Dan, I think it's a tire!"

She eased the car to a stop at the side of the deserted road and they watched the dust settle. Irish said, "It's a good five miles down the road to the ranch. I don't relish changing a tire, but it can't be an impossible task." He got out of the car.

"You shouldn't lift. I'll help." Tina scrambled out after him while Irish sorted through the keys looking for the one that would open the tool compartment.

"That's strange. I don't seem to have the key that opens this rear deck. It must be the ignition key." None of them worked. After doing everything he could think of, he said, "Well, this car's certainly burglarproof. How would the fair young lady like a nice walk? We could sit here on this road all day before another car comes along."

"You stay. I'll walk." She didn't sound very brave and he grinned at her.

"It isn't that bad." He turned to point across the hills. "Just over that next hill we'll be able to see the house. Come on, straight across country."

From the road the hills seemed to be rounded knolls studded with scrub pine and sage brush. It appeared logical to cut over the top of the first one.

When they reached the crest they stopped. "Well, that was a mistake," Irish admitted finally. The back side of the hill was a tilting ledge of crumbling rock, impossible to climb down. Its counterpart reared across the bowl-shaped meadow.

"It looks as if a giant broke a board across his knee and then buried the splintery ends in the ground," Tina said.

Irish studied the hillside and meadow. "This is oil country, Tina, and that's the type of terrain an oil man would love."

"Is this Bloomington's land?"

"Yes, the road is his southeast boundary. Well, let's get back to firm ground and cut around these hills. Be glad it's a cool day." He smiled down at her and reached for her hand.

In the meadow the grass was still green and long. Irish knew the summer's heat would soon dry the pools left by melting snow and then the grass would brown. "It takes a lot of land to raise cattle out here." He pointed to the grass. "In another month the livestock will be scrounging for the green stuff."

As they walked they crossed one section of grass that was curiously flattened and he turned to examine it. "Looks like tire marks. See? They head off through the meadow. Seems pretty marshy for a road."

"Let's follow them. Anything's better than these rocks." He glanced down at her sandals and nodded.

On a dry rise of land the marks stopped. "I guess one of Bloomington's trucks must have pulled in here, perhaps to drop feed. It looks like these tracks are pretty old. It's last season's grass that's been packed down. I guess it's logical to think he'd bring feed back in here for the cattle during the winter."

As they turned back toward the valley, Irish stumbled in the long grass and bent to see what his foot had struck. It appeared to be a piece of corroded pipe and he kicked it.

Surprisingly it fell apart and he picked up the shorter chunk. He discovered the surface of the cylindrical object was glazed and compacted as if it had been subjected to pressure.

Slowly turning the object, he noted the layers of different colors and textures. "Tina, I believe this is a drilling core." He looked down at the ground, moving his foot slowly through the grass. Some parts of the soil seemed to have been disturbed and then later trampled down.

"What is a drilling core?"

"One of the oldest and easiest methods of scouting for oil land is to drop a drill and cut out a core. It's like plugging a watermelon to see what's inside."

"So they study the inside of the earth," Tina said slowly, "and what does that core tell?"

"I don't know. I haven't any real knowledge of the oil drilling business. I have to rely on the expert's advice." He paused, "For whatever its merit, I think I'll hang on to a little chunk of this." He slipped the core into his pocket.

"Do you think Mr. Bloomington did this?"

"I hardly think so. He has absolutely no interest in oil wells. That's why he's selling the land the way he is."

"Dan, I can't quite understand all this. Is it right to refuse to develop oil land because of your own interests or because of some desire to just keep it all the way it was originally?"

"Right or wrong, you can't tell people how to live. Bloomington isn't dead set against the oil industry. When I first met him he told me that he believes there's a little oil on the land, but he doesn't want it tapped until it's absolutely necessary. Initially he indicated he'd tie up the mineral rights for a specified number of years before letting the landowner assume control of them."

"Don't landowners sometimes keep the mineral rights when they sell their land?"

"Yes, but Bloomington doesn't want to do that. He's an

old man without any close heirs, and he sees it only as a mass of legal red tape for a bunch of distant cousins."

For a while Tina walked in silence beside Irish. Abruptly she stated, "But Markham. I thought he was going along with Mr. Bloomington's wishes."

"I did too. He acted completely uninterested in the oil angle at the present time."

"Drilling cores don't indicate lack of interest."

"I was thinking the same thing. One could almost guess Mr. Markham knows more about this land than anyone gives him credit for knowing. Either that, or someone else came in and dropped the drill and then didn't like what he found."

"I'm confused. Is Mr. Markham a lawyer or a geologist?"

"Neither. He says he started out as an accountant in a little company which was later bought out by the outfit he works for now. He's just a Johnny-on-the-spot guy who's made himself indispensable by being there at the right time."

"He gives the impression of owning the company."

"That's probably why he's gone as far as he has." Irish grinned down at her.

Tina turned to face him. "What are you going to do now?"

Looking out over the grassland he thought about the question for a long time. He thought of Markham's careful avoidance of the slightest hint of unethical interest, and yet how determined he seemed to keep his company's name out of the picture. Also, there was that big retainer's fee. Uneasily he thought about the condominium and the leather furniture. Hadn't that fee given Markham license for his bold and heavy-handed demands?

"I think I know what the phrase means now." Tina looked puzzled and he explained, "The phrase, 'he's over a barrel'; it's an oil barrel and I know just how it feels."

"You think they've found oil?"

"I think they are certain enough it's there to make them willing to give a young green lawyer a big fat fee, much bigger than he's worth. Right now I'm trying to guess how they intend to get those mineral rights without a time clause attached, and I have the feeling I'm going to be the one to do it."

"And you really don't want to go against Bloomington's wishes? Well, what are you going to do?"

Irish turned to Tina, "What can I do? I've spent the money. Really, all I have to go on, besides this evidence, is only a vague uneasiness to indicate I don't believe Markham and his buddies are playing the game square."

"And you have the nice, honest face any old farmer would just automatically trust."

"Maybe my uneasiness is just indigestion." Something changed in Tina's expression. Before he could understand it, she turned away. Roughly he said, "I have the check. I intend to go over there and deliver it if I can get Bloomington to take it."

"Well, we'd better get on with it then." Tina's voice was cold and she quickened her steps. They walked in silence through the meadow, around the hill, and on through the sagebrush. There was one barbed wire fence to cross and then they rounded the slope that revealed the house.

"Is that it?" she asked. Irish nodded and they stopped to rest while they looked at the scene that lay before them. The green fields and orchards dotted with white buildings fused into a restful oasis to greet them after their dusty walk through the barren hills.

"It's a beautiful setting. It looks like a peaceful place to live; surely nothing unpleasant could ever touch it. I don't blame the Bloomingtons for wanting to keep it this way." Her voice was melancholy and Irish moved ahead.

The Bloomingtons saw them coming. The old gentleman limped from the chair on the porch and Mrs. Bloomington hurried from the house, wiping her hands on her apron.

Irish explained what had happened and surrendered his keys to Mr. Bloomington who headed for the field where the red tractor moved slowly up and down. While Irish and Tina sat on the veranda and drank lemonade, a blue truck detached itself from a cluster of outbuildings and moved down the road.

Irish watched the cloud of dust grow and hang over the road. Its rolling progress gave life to a scene that had been as intense and still as an oil painting. He wanted to share the impact of that peacefulness with Tina, but she was deep in conversation with Mrs. Bloomington.

Alone with his thoughts, Irish moved restlessly on his chair and tried to analyze the uneasy feelings that were surfacing in his mind, helped along, he decided, by the peace and almost unbelievable silence of this place.

It was the first time in his life he had experienced these rumblings of discontent. Moodily he stared at the drifting dust cloud.

Could it be that this growing restlessness was a symbol of fleeting youth, or did it have something to do with the accident? He only knew that the sharp appetite for life seemed to be slipping away from him. It was frightening. If life was to become a bore now, what would it be like in another ten years?

He glanced at Tina, watching her animated face as she talked to Mrs. Bloomington. But even as he looked and listened, he was becoming conscious of the fact that this feeling of discontent was too deep to be touched by Tina, a promising career, or even the peaceful life of this cattle ranch.

Appalled at the negative depths of his mood, he abruptly jerked himself erect in the chair. Tina and Mrs. Bloomington glanced at him and Mrs. Bloomington reached to pour more lemonade.

128

Carefully he settled back in the chair, determined to forget the feelings. He watched a spaniel gnawing a bone in the middle of the lawn. Once again he had the sensation of viewing this whole scene as if from a pinnacle, set apart and untouched by reality.

Markham had talked about his living here. He would be a gentleman farmer until . . . until what? He realized the until hadn't been specified.

The blue truck and the station wagon were coming back through the dust.

"We had to jimmy the lock," Bloomington explained. "It can't be locked now. Ed'll take a look at that tire for you."

After supper, while Tina went to help in the kitchen, Irish and Mr. Bloomington settled down to discuss the sale of the land. Irish shoved all thought of his discovery out of his mind and asked, "What kind of terms do you have in mind?"

Mr. Bloomington looked surprised and puzzled, "You said cash."

"Yes. I haven't changed my mind there. Mr. Markham indicated you had something else in mind—restrictions or clauses. I understand that you still hold the mineral rights." He thought of the drilling core that now lay in his suitcase.

Bloomington nodded. "That doesn't amount to much. And I can't see the sense of restrictions. They're just a bunch of red tape. I told Markham when I talked to him back in the beginning that I'm selling like this because I don't want no oil men messing up the place. They dig and scratch and whatcha' got when they're done? A nickel's worth of oil and all the good grazing land gone. Out here we're scared to death of erosion, and that's just what happens when you start cutting in. This is ranch country and I want to see it stay that way for a long time to come. Markham gave me his promise to keep it that way just as long as possible. A restriction don't mean much if your word isn't any good."

Irish sat stunned. As easy as that? Slowly he drew out the bank check. "Here's the earnest money and the contract. Now if you'll sign here, we'll get the ball rolling."

Later Bloomington stated, "Markham said you'd be the one to settle here for a while. Kinda' nice knowing it'll be in good hands. Think that back'll be up to it?

"Come on in here." Getting to his feet, Bloomington indicated the little room tucked under the stairs that he used as an office. Irish followed and the old man pulled a cane out of the gun cabinet. "There, bet you didn't know wood like this grew around here. My grandpa carved this out of a limb he found on the property. In the wintertime, back in those days, there wasn't much else to do after you'd got all the harnesses mended."

Irish protested, but Mr. Bloomington shook his head and insisted. "It's too long for me. Besides, I'd kinda' like to think of its staying here on the land where it belongs."

Early the next morning Tina and Irish drove back to Denver. Mr. Bloomington had the check and Irish had the signed papers.

Tina was silent most of the way home. The conversation they did have was superficial and stilted. Finally Irish was glad to lie flat in the back of the wagon, away from the necessity for small talk.

Back in Denver he left Tina at her apartment and went home. It was still early enough in the afternoon to contact Markham, but he discovered he was strangely reluctant to do so.

Pacing the floor in his living room, he found his thoughts going back to the drilling core and all the implications behind that discovery. Someone close to Bloomington was responsible for it, and, if the old man's candor hadn't convinced him of his honesty, the reasonable price he had put on his ranch would.

He fished the core out of his suitcase and set it on the table beside the recliner. There was only one other interested party involved as far as he knew, and that was Markham. Irish admitted that there were just too many things about the man that troubled him. "But," he reminded himself, "I have absolutely nothing concrete on which I can base an accusation. An old drilling core doesn't mean the man will run out and sink an oil well the day after the papers are signed."

His thoughts skirted the issue of the land and he found them returning to Tina. *How little she has said about it all*, he thought; *yet I've got the feeling she disapproves of the whole affair.*

He decided she was too uncompromising, rigidly uncompromising. He settled back in the recliner and adjusted his position. With his body at ease, his thoughts drifted.

From the beginning he knew everything about Tina pointed to a standard just a little higher than his. Wasn't she a little too puritanical? He remembered her response to his embrace. Caring or loving would apply to Tina, not puritanical. She seemed to care deeply about everything and everyone crossing her path. Humbly he decided that he wanted that caring to be for himself, always. Even as he acknowledged his desire, he realized he would have to do something to span the gap between them. Was her reluctance to discuss their relationship based on a deep moral difference? Not once had she condemned him for his actions, yet somehow he was aware of her disappointment in him at certain points.

Again he returned to the problem of the drilling core. The question became not, "What will Tina expect of me?" But instead, "What is right?" What would he want if he were in Bloomington's shoes? That settled it all.

He heaved himself upright in the chair and reached for the telephone. Glancing at his watch he was surprised to see the afternoon was almost gone.

He dialed the Wyoming area code and added the

Bloomington number. "Mr. Bloomington? This is St Clair. I've been doing a lot of thinking and I have a request to make. Hold that bank check until you hear from me again. The contract isn't valid until the check is cashed. No, it isn't a matter of money or deed, nothing from your end. I just need to do some more checking before this goes any farther. For your protection I request you hold the check."

He fingered the core and his discomfort grew as he listened to the old man's expression of admiration and confidence. He sighed with relief when he was able to replace the receiver.

Going to the kitchen, Irish made a pot of coffee and scrounged meat and cheese out of the refrigerator. As he buttered bread and smeared brown German mustard he was aware of the need to do a lot more thinking before he could call Markham. What was right and what was wrong?

There was expediency. He believed in that. Certainly the shrewd man was not to be condemned for digging his tunnel in the right direction and ignoring the side issues that could cause trouble.

He carried his coffee and sandwich back to the recliner. From the doorway he studied his room. The pale light of evening made hulks of the leather furniture and luminous shadows of the chrome and glass. Tonight his view of Denver was pink-striped sky and deep gray shadows pointed with light. Pleasant but lonely, he thought. He couldn't help remembering the shabby third floor apartment he had shared with Karen. The tiny rooms had been uncomfortably cramped, but while Karen was there it had seemed warm and full of life.

He set his supper on the end table and decided the sandwich looked like leftovers from last week—which it was. Slowly he sipped coffee and recited the usual lecture: "She's made her choice; be man enough to forget the past."

He tried to think about Tina, but the lonely memories persisted. Instead of trying again to anaylze the spot where it had all gone wrong, he let his memory dwell on the warmth and softness of Karen cuddled close. There were the whispered conversations that had always seemed best when done cheek to cheek. From the beginning home was where Karen had been.

He looked around the empty room and his anger toward her flared, fed by the old outrage of being discarded. Trembling, he ran restless fingers through his hair and wrenched his thoughts away from her. Even she had said the past couldn't be turned back.

Touching the button on the radio beside him, he tuned in music, lowered the volume, and resolutely picked up the stale sandwich.

Sometimes determination is born of dreams. During the night he awakened, his thoughts filled with Tina. Her steady blue eyes under the fluff of blonde hair seemed to be regarding him with an intensity that left him wide-eyed and questioning.

He and Tina. The combination was not only desirable, but also feasible. His time with Karen was finished. Tina would be the kind of a wife any ambitious attorney would be proud of. And, he admitted, she happened to be the wife this attorney wanted very much.

But would she want him? For the first time in his life, he rated himself by another person's standard. He realized he wasn't measuring up to what Tina would want in a husband.

He stood at the window and watched the morning paint the distant snowcaps with reflected pink. As the sky grew lighter he ticked off new goals. Number one, start divorce proceedings. That should have been done a year ago. Number two, discover what really made Tina what she was. He must understand her completely if they were to have a good marriage.

If he had a moment of uneasiness because his goals

seemed dispassionate and objective, the next moment brought satisfaction because he was being so mature about it all. He even grinned and shook his head over the memory of that hot-headed guy chasing Karen across the states, unwilling to take no for an answer. Life wasn't meant to be lived on emotion and impulse.

With determination he turned to the problem at hand: God. Going over the differences he had sensed in Tina, he realized his idea of God and Christianity didn't seem to have much in common with Tina's. With an amused grin he addressed the empty apartment. "Well, we'll just discover what you do believe. Tina, baby, perhaps we'll both need to change."

Sunday was no day to tackle Markham, but Sunday was the obvious day to get started on the other project.

He put on the coffee pot and dialed Tina's number. Her voice was startled and sleepy. For a second he wished he dared tell her of his hopes for the future. Caution made him stifle his enthusiasms for the day and he only asked, "Tina, how do you find out about God?"

The silence was long and heavy. He was surprised that she needed to study the problem. "For you I suppose you should read."

"What?"

"The Bible. Start with the New Testament."

"What part?"

"All of it. Start at the beginning."

Silence was deep on both ends of the wire. "Tina, give me a better answer. I've tried once and I was bored to death."

More silence, then, "Pray first. If you are really in earnest about the whole situation, I mean if you really want to learn, you'll have to tell Him that and expect Him to give you the desire and ability to understand. I'll pray too."

He was astonished and humiliated. Tina must think him some kind of a nut if she thought he couldn't get anything out of reading the Bible. "Well, of course."

He was still irritated as he concluded the conversation.
First breakfast, then he might as well get started.

As he ate bacon and eggs he thumbed through the
paper-backed Book. It was the New English Bible New Testament that he had picked up at the drugstore. Remembering Tina's advice, he decided it was ridiculous to think
common man couldn't read the number one best seller and
understand it.

He stacked his dishes in the sink and went to the recliner. Flipping the pages he estimated, with his ability to
read quickly, that he would be finished before evening.

As he settled deeper in the chair and turned to
Matthew, he remembered Tina's advice. It could make the
reading go faster. Closing his eyes, he found he was embarrassed and uneasy but he said the words with determination. "God, Tina said I'd need Your help to understand the
New Testament. I need to know about You." He hesitated,
remembering something from the past, perhaps a childish
prayer. He said the phrase, "In Jesus' name."

Stifling the first yawn generated by the ancestry of Jesus Christ and the familiar birth story, he closed his mouth
and saw, "Man cannot live on bread alone; he lives on every
word that God utters." He read on, wondering how mere
words would hold such sustenance.

Through Matthew he was beginning to see an impossible standard of goodness. Only curiosity kept him at it.
Surely the rest of the New Testament would offer more
than this. If it didn't, Tina must be the one to change her
mind.

When he finally rose and flexed his cramped muscles, he
realized he was hungry and went to fry more eggs in the
congealed fat still clinging to the skillet he had used that
morning.

Now the sun had moved westward and it was touching
the living room windows. Irish yawned and rubbed tired

eyes. Through the Gospels a picture was starting to emerge and he felt he was beginning to know intimately this Man Jesus. He muttered, "His favorite words are: 'How little faith you have, go and sin no more.' " Back with the Book, he experienced remorse and sadness, and he became a part of the crowd that stood by the cross. He felt like a spectator frozen in the pall of failure that surrounded that scene. The total picture was too intense; he dared not read on until he took one step away from the impact of it all. Objectivity, not emotionalism, he reminded himself.

Picking up the Book he continued to read, vaguely feeling as if he were in front of someone with whom he must argue. "It's just impossible to live up to all these ideas He's throwing out." Irish could admit that he was only an onlooker, sympathizing but not involved, and that was the way he wanted to keep it.

After he finished reading John, he sat trying to recall what he had just read, trying to understand it all. The impact of Jesus' willing crucifixion had been grasped back in Matthew, but now a new idea was generated out of John.

"I've never seen a guy who wanted friendship more than He did," he muttered soberly. "He was Creator. That's come through in the Gospel of John, and He's got the whole universe at His command; yet He's nursemaiding those disciples along like they're the most important people ever. He acts as if His whole goal in life is to have a deeply intimate relationship with them. He could have struck lightning bolts out of the air and had people bowing. But, instead, just like an ordinary man, He's out to win their friendship."

From some forgotten past he remembered a saying, "Jesus Christ is the same, yesterday, today, and forever." It was intriguing to ponder the possibility of the Christ still being interested in forming these close ties of friendship.

Realizing the emotional stance his thought had taken, he snorted at his notions. "Crazy ideas," he muttered. "Between that and talking to yourself, it's easy to see living alone doesn't agree with you."

He glanced at his watch. This was taking a great deal longer to read than he had anticipated. His annoyance disappeared as he flipped on the light and turned to Acts.

Irish was beginning to see a view of God that was staggering; the utter, complete fairness that allowed man freedom to be himself, whether or not that freedom would lead to Christ.

Humbly he read the fifth chapter of Romans and was confronted with the proof of God's love. Jesus Christ had died while man was still content with his sin.

Romans six talked about baptism and Irish settled comfortably. He was now on familiar territory. As he read his comfort vanished, and he was uneasily aware of a missing link. He put the Book down and thought back to that circumstance.

It said baptized into His death. Briefly he grinned. Surely that small, redheaded boy with the savagely pounding heart had fully expected death and resurrection—but that wasn't what was meant. He frowned and studied the words again. Was it possible there was a meaning or an affirmation that had been neglected in that rite?

Romans was completed. He was still puzzling over the verse that instructed him to let his mind be remade and his nature transformed. Now he was well into First Corinthians, reading with amused detachment about the misbehaving Corinthians, when suddenly he sat upright in the recliner. Simply, flatly, without qualifications, the Book instructed, ". . . and the husband must not divorce his wife."

He stared at the page, feeling as if he had received a shot of Novocain. Numbness was spreading into the new reservoir of feeling. He realized he wouldn't have felt the shock if he hadn't been so open, so willing to listen to the words.

"Well, brother Paul," he bitterly advised the page, "obviously you couldn't know the twentieth-century church wouldn't go along with your ideas."

He continued to read, but he was also thinking. Would

anyone on this earth be expected to take the advice of everything this Book taught? Surely there would be room for selectivity. Even as straight-laced as Tina seemed, she wouldn't go along with this new idea. Perhaps she didn't know about this section.

The beauty of Paul's writings caught him up in word pictures: Redeemed man was the incense offered to God by Christ; a letter written not with ink but with the Spirit; the more the grace of God is shared, the greater the chorus of thanksgiving ascending to God. Vulnerable, open to the beauty, he read, "The love of Christ leaves us no choice, when once we have reached the conclusion that one man died for all . . . men, while still in life, should cease to live for themselves, and should live for him. . . ." He ignored his churning emotions and hurried on.

As he continued, he became aware of the attractiveness of all he was reading, and then, abruptly, he encountered the fifth chapter of Ephesians with its statement: "Husbands, love your wives, as Christ also loved the church and gave himself. . . ."

Shoving the Book away, he buried his face in his hands. Why, when it was otherwise becoming so appealing, must this advice keep coming up? He rested, allowing his thoughts to drift. From the intense stillness in the very core of him, he began to wonder if his discontent would find answers in these pages.

It was a long time before he picked up the Book again, but doggedly he went on. In Philippians the Apostle Paul told of his heritage and achievements and Irish was conscious of a growing respect for the man, even as he rebelled against his teachings. But when Paul stated he counted his achievements as garbage in comparison to having Christ, Irish couldn't help reviewing his own life.

He thought of the shabby New York apartment and the mother with work-reddened hands who had held on to a dream of an education and a better life for her son.

His clearest memory of law school was pushing a broom

and waiting tables, and later dozing over books almost incomprehensible to his tired mind. But he had made it, and he couldn't conceive of listing his achievements as garbage regardless of the contrast.

While his thoughts were filled with Paul's comparison, his eyes stumbled ahead, but he was drawn back to read again: "Therefore since Jesus was delivered to you as Christ and Lord, live your lives in union with him. Be rooted in him; be built in him; be consolidated in the faith you were taught; . . . in Christ . . . you have been brought to completion."

Brought to completion? Wouldn't that mean no more of this restless pushing for something that couldn't be understood, let alone grasped?

Light had drawn a gray curtain across the window when he read in Hebrews that the Word of God is alive and it sifts the purposes and thoughts of the heart. Irish acknowledged that as truth.

Like a gentle hand scooping him up to hold him carefully were the words, "Their sins and wicked deeds I will remember no more at all . . . approach in sincerity . . . for the Giver of the promise may be trusted. . . . We have faith to make life our own. . . . Without faith it is impossible to please him."

Irish was reeling with fatigue but he couldn't put it down. Rubbing his eyes he read, "His divine power has bestowed on us everything that makes for life . . . enabling us to know the One who called us . . . through . . . his promises . . . you may escape the corruption . . . come to share . . . in the very being of God."

"The One who called us," his mind repeated, and he shook his head, trying to separate the words from the confusion his tiredness dictated. Again words surfaced and seared: "He is very patient with you, because it is not his will for any to be lost, but for all to come to repentance."

The sun was up and he turned off the lamp beside him.

He was unaware of all else until the last page was turned. The words were circling like matter caught in a whirlpool, but he couldn't discover their axis. With a supreme effort he lifted his weary body from the recliner and took one step. Cautiously he lowered himself, stretched across the rya rug and was immediately asleep.

Chapter 10

While Irish slept the sun moved across the sky. Its warmth, blazing through the western window, awakened him. He opened one eye to the blinding rays and rolled on to his stomach.

Light. He was called the Light. Was this searing comfort like the light Jesus was? This warmth that went all through him, easing the ache, chasing the night shadows. Could that be compared to possessing Christ? He remembered and could almost quote the words. It was something about walking in the light as He is in the light and being cleansed by the blood of Jesus.

Idly he wondered how long it would take the piercing clarity of the words he had read to fade from his mind. In peace, he drifted toward sleep again.

The warmth was as real as a presence and, as he hovered close to sleep, it was as if the folds of his mind relaxed and spread open, visible and instructing. The Book had been talking about a relationship, not a religion. How attractive was the total picture, yet there were the hard things Jesus had said. Jesus had cautioned His would-be followers with the illustration that no man builds a house without first counting the cost. That was fair. Don't leap before you look.

What did it mean to daily pick up your cross and follow?

He was awake now. He rolled into the shade and thought about it all. What was sin? Could it be many different things? In that moment he accepted the fact that the worst sin of all was to be faced with all that he had read during the past twenty-four hours and then to turn his back on it. Friendship with Jesus Christ became the most appealing thing he had ever considered.

He discovered the words whole and complete; waiting only to be said, and he said them: "His divine power has bestowed on me everything I need to know. It makes me able to know the One who is calling. Through Jesus' redemptive act I may escape the corruption and share in the very being of God, the One who calls."

He took a deep breath and recognized the failure of his baptism. "Now I die," he said slowly, "so that in Christ I may be made alive. I didn't realize before that it is a real death, a death that leaves behind the old and goes on to the new. Now I'm ready for that."

He felt as if his whole body was filled with the burden of wanting to enter that friendship. Abruptly he recalled the sections he had rejected.

He opened his eyes to the blinding sun. Karen. Could turning his mind off to those sections somehow prevent his entering the relationship?

God's Word said he must not divorce his wife; that he must love her as dearly as Christ loved the church. Give himself for his wife?

Bitterness filled him and the irony of it all twisted his face until he rubbed his aching jaw. Was Tina, who had brought him to the new way with her sweetness and promise, now to be denied? He contemplated some giant mystical leap that would clear this hurdle and give him Jesus Christ and Tina too.

Instinctively he knew Tina wouldn't go along with that. He was beginning to understand the unhappiness in her eyes; the things she had hinted about, saying he must discover them for himself. Jesus Christ had been the invisible barrier between the two of them.

He buried his face in the crook of his sun-seared arm and wrestled with the bitterness. It was as if the whole affair with Karen had been locked deeply inside and now it must all come out. He trembled with anger and frustration and began to realize how deeply his feelings for her had turned in upon themselves and had become warped and twisted.

The revelation astonished him and he wondered how he could have treated her so casually, even with friendliness. Surely that attempted kiss had been no mockery, or had it?

He tried to dismiss the thoughts and go back to his original line of thinking. In all honesty he had to acknowledge that the yearning desire, which had been growing all night, was a desire for all that Jesus Christ held out to him. But there were some hard parts.

He went back over them. Deny himself and have a daily walk with God. The desire he felt growing outweighed the sacrifice and he waited, conscious now of only the unsatisfied hunger. The clock ticked away the minutes and the patch of sunlight moved slowly.

Irish finally got to his feet and went to the recliner. He glanced at the clock and thought he should call Markham, but a strange inertia held him powerless and uncaring for anything except that burning spot of restlessness that had been his constant companion since yesterday.

The patch of sunlight was plastered against the dining room wall when out of the depths of his inward search he tried to form words, hoping to break the bond of misery he felt. The words that came to his lips were out of the buried memory of a small boy.

"Our Father which art in Heaven, Hallowed be Thy name. Thy kingdom come. Thy will be done, in earth, as it is in heaven. Give us this day our daily bread. And forgive us . . . as we forgive . . ." he stopped. Karen's face was before him.

He felt the divine circle tightening. To be forgiven and reconciled to God was a need that gnawed until he knew without forgiveness he couldn't continue to live. He and Karen before God. The bitterness was sickening. Leaning back in the recliner he gave himself to it; it swept him, possessed him.

The room grew dim with approaching night and finally he could say aloud, "Jesus Christ, You know I want this union with You more than life. You also know I can't forgive Karen. Is there anything You can do about this?"

He remembered a verse he had read. It was something about casting his cares on God because God cared. With fatigue-numbed lips he muttered, "I throw it on You. I'm willing to let You help me if You will."

It was nearly midnight when Irish got out of the recliner. He felt as if the room were an illusion. It seemed his numbed feet couldn't comprehend the floor, or his hands the leather. Swaying in the middle of the room, he rubbed his hands over the stubble on his chin.

Wondering where the hours had gone, he moved slowly toward the bathroom. As he stood under the steaming needles of water and felt its ministry on the scars down his spine, he began to feel life coming back. He turned on the cold water and the shock of it couldn't compare with the shock of new life he felt. When he stepped out of the shower and reached for the towel, even the soles of his feet tingled with something he interpreted as total confidence and absolute relief.

He marched into the kitchen aware of a roaring hunger, but standing with the refrigerator door open, he stared at only eggs and tomatoes. Shoving that idea aside, he shut the door and began to pace the floor. Conscious, logical thought was impossible. Suddenly, he was tired and he turned toward the bedroom, only dimly aware that it had been almost forty hours since he had left that room.

Overnight a new way of life started for Irish. The next morning he sat on the edge of the bed and addressed Jesus Christ. "Okay, this business with Karen is the worst I'll ever have to face. I don't know how to handle it, but I'm free from the strangle hold it's had on me. It's in Your hands. Your Word tells me to let the Spirit direct and I intend to do that. Just please, let me know loud and clear what You want. I'm new at this game. With Karen, I don't know. With Markham, I don't have any doubts."

For breakfast he finished off the last six eggs and ate three tomatoes, whole. Bending over the sink he let the seeds and juice run off his chin in a way that he hadn't done since the last time his mother had caught him at it.

He felt like singing and didn't know a song. From long-forgotten days there was the doxology. He stood in the middle of the kitchen, wiping tomato juice with the dish towel and shouting off key, "Praise God from whom all blessings flow."

Later that morning, when he marched into Markham's office, he realized he wasn't wearing the back brace. That caused an astonished grin and Markham saw it. "Well, St Clair, that looks like success. I was a little apprehensive. Tried to call you this weekend, but I guess you were out."

Only briefly Irish puzzled over that before he shrugged and followed the man into his office. While he carefully watched Markham's face, he told about the flat tire and the hike across the ranch to the Bloomingtons' house.

"We followed tire tracks thinking they'd lead up to the house. They were old ones." He deliberately emphasized the words. "They dead-ended on a nice dry knoll. When we turned to walk back, I stumbled on this." He rolled the drilling core across the desk.

Markham leaned back in his chair. "Well, Danny boy, it looks like someone's trying to steal our thunder." His small, hard eyes challenged him and for a moment Irish hesitated.

Leaning forward he placed his hands flat on Markham's desk and said, "Didn't anyone ever tell you that you're to level with your attorney? You might get by with cheating the IRS and bilking the FBI, but your attorney, no."

"So, what's the deal? You didn't get paid enough?"

"Cut it out, Markham. I don't like clients sneaking around the back door, dropping drill bits on somebody's land. There aren't too many rigs around that country. I don't think its going to be too hard to find a guy who remembers dropping a drill on Bloomington's land about six or eight months ago."

Markham's gaze shifted quickly. "You didn't think I'd be stupid enough to take that much of a gamble on a piece of land, did you? That land looks lousy unless you happen to know about the one little valley. It was just too easy to pass up. Don't be stupid about this."

He grinned and reached for his hip pocket. "So what do you need? That little nurse giving you a bad time?"

"Out, Markham, out." Irish swallowed his anger and snapped his fingers.

Markham rubbed his slack jaw. "Now that's ridiculous at this stage of the game. Come on, Danny boy, there's too much at stake."

"Pretty good oil land?"

"I thought you'd already guessed that." The man's grin was confident and then his jaw tightened. "Name it, we'll talk business. I'm going to have that land."

"I want out," Irish repeated. "I intend to tell Bloomington that the deal's off and why."

"Your accusations will never hold up in court."

"Court? What makes you think I'd take that route? Right now I don't have a leg to stand on myself." Moving by instinct now, he said slowly and deliberately, "And I don't think you do either."

He continued to watch Markham's eyes as he said, "You retained me in good faith." He was feeling his way along the facts, the honest ones. "You let Bloomington believe you were only interested in raising cattle out there right now. You let me believe it was purely a gamble, a speculation of the most dubious sort."

On sudden impulse, Irish asked, "Your company isn't in on this, is it?" Now the man's bold expression faded. He shook his head. "No, it was just a last ditch stand by an old man who's lost his usefulness to the firm. You have to be in my position to know the stupid, desperate things you can dream up."

Now Irish could see him as he was, and he knew it was a tired, old man hiding behind that blustery personality. He felt sorry for him. He pulled a chair close to the desk and sat down facing Markham. "Look, Markham, this just isn't right. I gave Bloomington the check and got his signature on the contract." Markham's head jerked and he straightened. Irish hurried on. "But after I got home I had some more thinking to do. I called Bloomington and asked him to hold the check. At the time I didn't know what I'd do. See, I've got plenty at stake too. I'm a young attorney on the way up. Also, I've spent the retainer fee, which by the way, is the thing that made me suspicious. It was just too big."

Irish was silent, caught for a moment in wondering how he would repay the money. He glanced at Markham and took a deep breath. That wasn't the important thing.

"Mr. Markham, I've had quite an encounter with Jesus Christ this weekend. It all started when I began wondering about the dividing line between right and wrong. I've always considered myself honest. At least honest enough not to be caught in the wrong. One twenty-four-hour exposure to God's Word convinced me I didn't have any moral basis for judging right or wrong."

Abruptly Markham got to his feet. "You want out," he said tersely. "Well, you got it. Forget the retainer. You did your job. It's yours to keep." His hard eyes signaled his advantage and Irish knew the implications behind the generosity; he would still be Markham's man.

He shook his head. "No, I knew enough to make me guilty almost from the beginning. It wouldn't be right."

After Irish left Markham's office he continued downtown to his own modest office. As he inserted the key in the lock he heard his name. "St Clair, old man, you back at it?"

It was Allen Kincaid, a fellow attorney. He clapped Irish gently on the shoulder. "Man, we've missed you. Say, Michaelson is still looking for a corporation man, if you're interested."

Irish was touched by the concern. The nagging worry his empty desk generated disappeared. "Kincaid, I appreciate it and I may go see him. That checking account is getting a little thin. In a couple of weeks I should be back in the running again."

Kincaid nodded and went on to his own office. Irish dusted the top of his desk, collected a pile of correspondence and relocked the door.

Back at the apartment, Irish stared at the unopened pile of letters and thought about Tina. He dared not probe his emotions, but he was aware of the need to talk to her and let her know of all that had happened since their conversation.

"Cut it off, old man," he advised himself, "the sooner, the better, and make it clean and quick. In the final analysis it won't hurt as much." He stared at the rug between his feet and knew that wasn't the truth. Hurt? It would probably hurt the rest of his life.

He glanced at his watch and saw there were three hours before Tina would be off duty. Resolutely he looked around and saw the things that demanded attention.

First the dieffenbachia. He watered the plant and picked up scattered newspapers. There was the pile of clean shirts the laundry had left and there were dishes to be washed. Through it all he was conscious of avoiding the thoughts that needed to be shaped into a decision that wouldn't hurt Tina.

When he finally picked up the phone, he was no nearer that decision. She answered and he asked, "Tina, how about dinner?"

There was a long silence and finally, "Well, did you take my advice?"

"Yes."

"All of it?"

He was puzzled, "Yes, but what's that got to—"

"Then I don't think we should, do you?"

It took a while for it all to sink in. He took a deep breath, "You're guessing at my reaction."

"I'm not wrong, am I? Dan, you were obviously looking for answers. I had enough faith in you to believe that once you really started looking, there could be only one response—total obedience."

Her voice broke, but he had to ask, "How do others get around it?"

"I don't know, Dan. I only know what's right for me. I think you're convinced too. You know, your decision was what I really wanted all along. But I've made a mess of everything. I suppose I must admit God has been warning me against intruding in your life. I've made some terrible, selfish mistakes, but I've learned too. Dan, I'm sure God hasn't given up on Karen. Can't you please—" her voice trailed away.

He replaced the receiver, feeling as if it were suddenly too heavy for his tired hand. The paper-backed New Testament still lay beside the phone. Its cover was creased and every page showed evidence of being touched. You can't go back, he reminded himself. There isn't such a thing as going back, only on and on. He frowned, trying to remember who had expressed that thought with such a great deal of sadness.

He reached for the Book. Thumbing through the pages, he read again those hard passages, trying to see some hope. When his hand slipped, the pages turned and again he read the final statement in Matthew: "And be assured, I am with you always, to the end of time."

It was another two days before he got around to opening the mail he had brought from his office. There was a solicitation for money; he dropped it in the wastebasket. He opened an invitation to join the Cherry Hills Country Club, and it went into the wastebasket too. The rest were bills. Wondering how he could have accumulated the stack of gasoline bills, he thumbed through them. He noticed Karen's signature on some of them and realized she must be using his credit card.

Separating them according to signatures, he picked up Karen's and began sorting them by the date. When he finished he went through them again and was surprised to see the picture they drew.

Spreading them on the table he stared at them. Even in his indecision to allow God to control his whole life, he hadn't expected something as concrete as this. With Karen's disappearance he had considered the matter totally out of his hands. Now, as clearly as if he were following a road map, her path lay before him.

He fingered the cards and read: Morrison, Fairplay, Poncha Springs. She must have stopped to ask directions at Poncha Springs, he decided. Surely she wouldn't need gasoline that soon. Next it was South Fork. He wondered if she had trouble on Wolf Creek Pass; he was uneasy, thinking about the unreliable little vehicle. The next day's ticket was from Pagosa Springs and he breathed a sigh of relief. The next two tickets were marked Homer's Corner and they were dated two weeks apart. The story told by the bills was intriguing, but he ignored all the implications and reached for his checkbook.

After he had totaled the checks he studied the balance and looked around the room. With that thin figure and the retainer to be returned, there was only one decision to make. Would it be possible to squeeze all that leather furniture and the queen-sized bed into an apartment as small as the one he and Karen had shared? He tried to visualize it, and then he looked around to see what he could get rid of.

The dieffenbachia could find a home elsewhere. His eyes lingered on the plant. Its arrogance seemed suited for the leather and chrome but he wondered about Karen's choice. She had filled their old apartment with geraniums, crimson, and something she called apple blossom, and there had been squatty lemon-scented candles on the red linen covered table. That apartment had been an echo of Karen's warmth. Why had she bought dieffenbachia instead of geraniums?

He shrugged off the question and reached for the phone book. Clarence Crowley, his real estate buddy, would take care of the condominium and would also find him a smaller place.

As he waited for his call to be placed, he thought about Clarence and his sister Freddie. It had been Freddie who had taken Karen under her wing and had found a place for her in her own fashion design studio. He shook his head over Freddie. She was as unpredictable as Colorado weather and as volatile as the frequent thunderstorms. At times he had regretted the alliance his own eagerness had started. For some time he had wondered if Karen's relationship with Freddie had been as smooth as she had always led him to believe.

Clarence came on the line and he explained his need and instructed the man to place the condominium on the market.

He was still thinking about Freddie after he hung up. In recalling the different situations in which he had seen her, he remembered the overwhelming feeling of power and force in the woman. She was the typical liberated woman on her way up, and "up" was one step higher than all the males around her. "Overbearing" was a good word for her. He was momentarily amused by the vision of a cat called

Freddie pouncing on everything that moved.

It was the next afternoon when Freddie called. He had been doing the strenuous exercises the doctor had prescribed. Leaning against the kitchen wall he mopped perspiration from his face with the dish towel and listened to Freddie. As he tried to control his heavy breathing, he decided that Freddie didn't punctuate her sentences with periods, only commas. There were no question marks; just demands with no room for answers.

He listened. She had seen Clarence, she informed him, and knew he was giving up his apartment and she was interested in seeing it and she knew Karen had been in town, because she knew he had been in an accident and she assumed Karen had told him about the baby and that was why she left and she wanted to see the apartment as soon as possible and did Clarence have a key yet? He mopped his whirling head. There was one word that was important.

"Freddie!" he shouted and couldn't believe the silence. "You said baby," he said slowly.

She recovered, "Oh, I thought you knew all about it. Irish, old boy, I'm not about to divulge secrets, no sir. You just go ask her if you want to know and leave the key with Clarence." The receiver clicked.

Irish looked down at the phone in his hand. His mind tried to grapple all the possibilities that word suggested. Could it be that he had a child somewhere? A child, his son. He visualized a small, redheaded boy. Where was the child? There was his emphatic decree of no children. Cringing he recalled his hard words. Could that explain Karen's abrupt departure two years ago?

For a long time he stared at the silent phone while memories rose like bubbles in his mind. Finally he moved and sighed heavily. It was surprising how much his feelings had changed during the past two years, surprising and sad. Had they changed too late? He shook off the heavy questions. It was highly possible Freddie didn't know what she was talking about. It was just as possible she was deliberately provoking him with twisted facts. But sitting here wouldn't settle any of the questions.

With a sigh he slowly got to his feet. He knew there was only one person with the answers. The credit card receipts were the map. That would lead him to her.

Chapter 11

It was the third week of May. With the promise of summer, business at the cafe was picking up, and Karen frequently found herself filling in at the tackle counter and gas pumps. Since Jonathan had left Amy with her grandmother, Letty seldom helped at the cafe. But Karen found she didn't mind the extra busy schedule.

On the day Homer and Letty went into Pagosa Springs, taking Amy and her great-grandfather, Karen and Rosemarie had the cafe to themselves. It was the afternoon lull and while Rosemarie clattered about in her domain, Karen leaned on the cash register and sleepily stared out the window.

The last mound of snow hidden in the shadow of the spruce had disappeared. The meager sunshine of avalanche lilies had been replaced by flaming Indian paintbrush and the shadow colored lupine.

Through the front windows of the cafe, Karen could see the subalpine daisies and marsh marigolds growing in clumps along the ditch bank across the road from the restaurant. Only barbed wire strung on graying posts kept foraging cattle from making a dinner of the flowers. The door was open to the damp, cowy, mountain breeze that Karen associated with the area as much as she did the sound of soft mooing backed by the gurgle of icy water over smooth stones.

She had been watching the cars pass on the graveled road. Men with fishing poles and fly-studded hats, women in scarves and sun hats, and tousled-topped youngsters hanging out the windows were the most common sights this time of year.

A blue station wagon slowed, crossed the parking lot and stopped at the gas pumps. With a sigh Karen got off the stool and pulled her flowered, percale dress straight. "Gas," she called to Rosemarie. "I'll get it."

On her way around the car she unlatched the gas hose. "Yes?" she questioned. When the occupant of the car didn't answer, she turned. It was Irish looking as if he couldn't believe his eyes. He studied every detail of her face, her percale dress, and even the reddened hands holding the hose.

"I don't need gas." He got out of the car and, as she slowly replaced the hose, he was watching her with a quizzical expression she found more difficult to endure than all his former indifference.

She took a shaky breath and said, "If you don't want gas, you can't park in front of the pumps." He nodded and got back into the car.

She waited beside the pumps while he parked. The sun was hot on her back and shoulders, and the mingled odors of grease and gasoline were making her light-headed. When he walked back to her she was conscious only of the pop of gravel under his feet.

"Karen, I want to take you home." Startled, she raised her head to stare at him, completely unable to believe he meant it. His expression was deeply serious. No, she decided, studying him more closely, troubled. He continued to look at her as if he were really seeing her for the first time.

She swallowed and moistened her lips. "No, Irish," her voice was only a whisper, "I'm happy here."

"And you can't face a temporary unhappiness in an effort to make a wrong right?"

She puzzled over his words before slowly answering, "That's what I tried to do before, but I couldn't get past the unhappiness. What about Tina?"

"That's over. Finished. Remember the past can only be forgotten."

She shook her head slowly. "I thought so, but in reality that isn't right. The past colors the present, on and on. It makes the present. Irish, I don't want to go back. I'm happy here." Resolutely she straightened her shoulders and declared, "You're the same old, hard-headed Irish. All you want to do is give orders and you want me to jump to obey. I have a surprise for you. I'm not jumping."

She waited for his retort. He frowned and chewed his lip. He looked as if he had a great deal to say and didn't know where to begin. Glancing around he said, "I absolutely will not take no for an answer until you've heard me out."

She couldn't help the little gasp. "I haven't heard you this determined since Kansas City. You're supposed to snap at me and then back down and give me the silent, little-boy act."

"Perhaps that's why there's been trouble. My immaturity has drawn lines between us that I didn't know were there."

Knowing that wasn't the trouble, she felt the wilting inside. The sun seemed to have lost its power to warm and she whispered, "No, Irish, that isn't so. But don't push me."

"I won't, Karen," his voice was unexpectedly gentle. "Just hear me out."

She glanced toward the cafe. "I'm working now. You can't hang around."

"I'll have a sandwich and come back later. When do you get off work?"

She shrugged, "Who knows? When Homer and Letty come back."

"You don't keep very regular hours?" She shook her head and walked through the door ahead of him.

Rosemarie was standing behind the counter. With hands wide spread on the smooth surface, she leaned forward and watched Irish with obvious interest.

"This is Irish, Rosemarie," she muttered waving her hand. Irish slid onto the stool nodding. "Rosemarie'll get you something to eat." She retreated to the cash register.

Irish ordered and with a sardonic grin asked, "Will the management let me buy that little lady a cup of coffee?"

The curiosity in Rosemarie's eyes was very evident but she grinned at him and poured two coffees. After she slapped the hamburger down in front of him, she went back to the kitchen.

Reluctantly Karen slid onto the stool beside him. She shoved the catsup toward him and his hand brushed hers. He was still watching her with that strange, still expression. Puzzled she tried to analyze it. He seemed to be curious about her but underneath there was a deep, painful questioning in his eyes that completely baffled her.

"Did the Volkswagen break down?" She shook her head and watched him bite into the sandwich. After another bite, "Did you have a hard time getting over Wolf Creek Pass?" Again she shook her head and tore her fascinated gaze away from his face. She sipped the bitter coffee and miserably wished he hadn't come.

The bell on the screen tinkled and she looked over her shoulder as Homer, Letty, and Amy came through the door. The child ran toward Karen screaming with excitement. Beside the stool she bounced. Holding a tiny baby doll up, she tried to scramble up on the stool.

Homer crossed the room and lifted Amy. Impatiently Letty said, "She's only trying to show you her new dolly." Amy poked a diminutive nursing bottle at the plastic lips and laughed with glee. Karen leaned against the counter and tried to smile at the child, but inside she could feel the discomfort growing into misery. She saw the hard, questioning look Irish gave her before he turned to Homer and Amy.

Karen managed introductions, and slid off the stool. Leaving Irish to cope with the situation, she picked up his empty plate and headed for the kitchen.

Rosemarie's eyes were bright with curiosity and she asked, "Some pest?"

"Oh, so, so," Karen murmured. "Depends on how you look at it. I've known him for some time."

When she returned to the counter Homer said, "Take off. You've been here since six-thirty this morning."

As they left the restaurant, Irish asked, "Where do you live?"

"With Homer and Letty. They had a spare room."

"Let's ride. You can point out some of the sights."

"I need to change. Wait here and I'll be back in a few minutes." Karen slipped through the trees to the log house. As she walked up the steps she wondered how she could cope with Irish without having to explain her past to these people. Somehow the two worlds wouldn't mesh, and she didn't want the emotional upset of seeing Irish's sophistication belittling Homer's black Book or Aunt Sarah's funny, loving ways.

Gramps was in the kitchen, nodding in the rocker beside the cold cook stove. She changed into shirt and jeans and paused beside his chair. "There's a fellow here I've known for ages. I'll probably be late so tell Letty not to wait." On impulse she pressed a kiss against the soft white hair.

"Now you behave yourself," his eyes held the concern that she had been seeing more often. "We don't want you lolly-gagging off from us."

As she walked back to the parking lot, she wondered if her reluctance was a self-protective desire to avoid seeing that love leave Gramps' eyes if she were to reveal her relationship to Irish.

She slid into the front seat of the station wagon and Irish asked, "Where can I find a room around here?"

She thought about that. "You mean you're planning on staying here?"

He gave her a quick glance and from his silence she guessed he didn't like her response. "Where does this road go?"

She shrugged, "No place in particular. It follows the stream, goes past a few farms and on up into the trees. It dead-ends pretty close to the ruins of an old mining town. Not much to see except for a few old buildings." She glanced at him. "It's a pretty good hike and I doubt you could make it with your back." She could see that rankled, but she didn't care.

He headed up the graveled road and they rode in silence. He had his head against the door frame as if listening to the music the stream made. Here spruce and fir cast deep shadows across the road. At the edge of the farmland the trees were poplars and cottonwood, and the road dipped back and forth between them and the stream.

They passed the farm where Amy had scampered with the lambs. Beyond the house was a white painted sign nailed to a tree and Irish slammed on the brakes. "They have cabins," he explained heading down the road to the house.

"Irish, don't!" Karen exclaimed in dismay. "I don't want you to stay. Go back to Denver where you belong."

He stopped the car and turned to her. "I intend to stay. Karen, I have a great deal to say to you and it must be said. Don't run away, because now I'll chase you to the ends of the earth. Let me have my say and then the choice will be yours."

He left the car and went to the house. While he was gone Karen pondered over the strange new gentleness she sensed in him. He returned and pointed the car down a rutted road angling through the trees. The cabin was log with a stone chimney. Momentarily Karen was enthralled by the doll house quality of it.

While Irish carried his suitcase inside, Karen went to stand in the doorway. There was a puffy bed with a patchwork quilt and a tiny iron stove in the corner. "I'll bet that's a feather bed," she went to poke. "It'll ruin your back."

"Forget my back," he said irritably. He thumped the suitcase in a corner and pried open a window. "This'll do. Come on, unless you'd rather sit here and talk." She shook her head and followed him back to the car.

"What about your office?"

"I've no intention of going back until the middle of June. Right now I think two weeks in the mountains is the best therapy for an ailing back."

They reached the end of the road and Irish parked beside the stream. He pointed to the tumbled logs. "An old bridge?" She nodded and he added, "I suppose that cut marks the old road up to the mining camp. That would be a wild one to go down in a wagon loaded with ore. Want to hike up there?"

Karen shook her head. They walked to the edge of the stream. "It's pretty clear now. A couple of weeks ago we were up here and the stream was muddy from the runoff."

"We?" he questioned.

"Jonathan, Homer's son. He's a public school teacher in Denver. He's also Amy's father."

"Where's her mother?" It was said evenly but the underlying feeling made Karen turn and look at Irish.

"She died of cancer over a year ago. Forget the innuendos. Neither of us is interested in the things that everyone else thinks about when they see a male and female together." He relaxed and she was even more puzzled.

Irish started for the logs and Karen noticed his back. "Aren't you wearing your brace?"

"No, I've been getting along without it for the past week. I have it with me, mostly because I didn't know what effect driving would have on me."

"Well, let's not try the mining camp. I don't want to be responsible for any more damage." He seemed satisfied and they sat on the edge of the old bridge with their feet dangling only inches from the frothing water.

"I wish we'd done more of this type of thing," Irish said soberly as he looked at her. "Just being together more often might have been the thing our marriage needed."

She couldn't help stiffening and pulling away from him and he noticed. Quickly, he added, "Karen, I've changed. I'm sorry for the failure of our marriage and I really do forgive you."

She turned so suddenly she almost slipped from the log and he reached to steady her. Shrinking away from his hand, she asked, "Forgive, what do you mean?"

He turned a startled face toward her, and as she pondered her words, wondering what emotion that sentence revealed, she saw his puzzled expression change to alarm and then flare into anger. Abruptly the anger died and she watched him lower his head and stare at the water.

It was a long time before he spoke again, and Karen huddled on the logs with her arms clasped about herself, trying to shut out a miserable chill.

"Karen," he spoke slowly, as if he must study every word he uttered, "I've become a Christian. Everything is changed. I don't even think the same way I did before. I don't have the same values. Do you believe that is possible?"

When he looked at her, she couldn't keep back the surging bitterness. "But Irish, dear, you always were a Christian. You've never failed to impress me with that idea, that holier than thou idea."

He winced, "I didn't realize you felt that way. But no, Karen, I don't mean it's something I've accomplished. It's something done for me. I suppose most of us consider ourselves Christian. That is, we belong to a church and have a pretty good idea of what is required of us. But, Karen, I've discovered there's a very real difference between saying you're a Christian and really being one.

"Karen, when I was a little kid I was baptized, and I thought it took care of the whole matter for the rest of my life. Now I've discovered that's all just meaningless ritual unless it goes deeper than that. I've been reading the New Testament, and now I see that being a follower of Jesus Christ demands a change that starts with the inner man and ends with the whole manner of living."

Karen watched the play of expression across Irish's face. She saw the earnestness as he tried to find words to express himself, and was fascinated as she watched sorrow and joy mingle on his face to hint of his inward struggle as he told of his battle. As if in a dream, at a point where she couldn't be touched by it all, she heard him sum it all up with his words, "Karen, honey, nothing is as important in life as this deeply personal experience with Jesus Christ. It's life itself. It's moving out of the plane of indifferent, marginal living, called religion, into a vibrant relationship with your God."

Karen didn't know how long she had been shaking her head, but abruptly Irish demanded, "Why are you doing that?"

"That isn't so. Irish, you're living on a purely emotional plane. I know. I've spent two years learning the right way. You're only making a mood of surrender." Her voice was mocking, "Where is the nice, calm, objective Irish? How did you happen to be caught up in wild emotional experiences? Your way is the old-fashioned, ineffectual way. That kind of religion is hopelessly out of date. You need to be enlightened and, my dear Irish, I intend to do it."

He turned and draped one leg over the log he was sitting on. Facing Karen, he asked, "Where did you get the idea it's out of date?"

"It's obvious. Religion has been failing almost since its invention. Man can't cope with the rules and regulations."

"I know, Karen," he broke in eagerly. "That's just what I discovered. God gave a clear picture of right and wrong through His law, and—"

"And isn't that a terrible view of God?" She allowed her voice to drip with scorn. "A God who would demand impossible things. See, that's where the failure is." Karen paused. The expression on Irish's face had changed to one of almost amusement. Momentarily she faltered.

"Go on," he urged, "I'm listening."

"The master said the true spirit of religion is lacking when it stresses only right and wrong, creating only a fear of punishment and hell." She couldn't help shivering as she added, "Creating the fear of God in the mind of man, oh, what a cruel idea!"

"And what's the better way?"

"To take away the fear of hell, to transcend the gross levels of man and his ideas of God. Instead of spending all this time thinking about Him, you should transcend the whole level of living, learn how to escape the gross, and then enter into the direct experience of eternal Being."

"Through meditation?"

"Yes, in this way you experience Being."

"Then I take it you're still meditating."

"A little. I don't have enough time." She was silent for a long time. Picking at the lichen on the log she tried to think of a way to make Irish understand it all. It was becoming very important. He prodded her arm.

"Irish, you don't experience God, Being, in an emotional way. That's gross, not faith. In meditating you enter into a great quietness, and you only know you've been there by the peace and happiness you feel when you come out."

"You keep using the term 'gross.' What do you mean?"

"It's all that you experience through the senses. The human part of man, not the spiritual. Anyway, when you meditate all the time, you just automatically get to the place where things go right. You don't have to worry about making the right decisions; they're automatic. But the biggest thing is knowing how you're being used. See, when you practice meditating all the time, you become a tool in the hands of the divine. You are being used to spread joy and peace and happiness to all."

"And that's what you're doing now?" She picked at the lichen again. He held out his arms and he was laughing at her, "Then come here and spread a little joy and happiness."

She scooted away from him, "You're being gross."

"Then everyday living doesn't have anything to do with meditating and spreading joy."

"Yes, it does. That's why I came back to Denver when I heard you were in the hospital. I knew my mission must be to destroy the old karma and bring happiness to you at that time. See, Irish, this is all caught up in the eternal existence of things, the unending cycle."

"Come again?"

"Life repeats. You live and die and live again, over and over. How you live now determines what you'll be in the next life."

"Reincarnation. What's the purpose of it all?"

"To spread enough happiness, to benefit mankind to the place where you can finally escape the whole cycle and evolve into Being."

"Heaven?"

"No, I don't really know what it is like. No one does. You're just taken into it."

"Jesus said He was going to prepare a place for us," Irish stated. "That sounds pretty concrete and clearly outlined."

"Irish, this all isn't in conflict with religion. It's supposed to be a way to make religion better. A success where there's been nothing but failure before. Don't be childish about it all. And just don't expect an emotional daddy-son relationship with God. That's the illusion."

"What does meditation teach about Jesus Christ?"

"That He was successful in finding the kingdom within himself just like all the other great teachers, Buddha and the others."

"But God's Word teaches Jesus Christ is God. If meditation puts Him on the same level as Buddha, then there's something terribly wrong with meditation."

"I know the importance of the peace I've found and nothing can take it away. I'm convinced of the rightness of all this. Can't you see? Irish, I've been taught that through my thought and actions I can produce good for you as well as for myself. See, the influence of karma—that's my activity influenced through my mind by the Being—will someday create harmony and rhythm with the cosmic life, and then I'll be able to do all good by being all good. That's why I came back to Denver, to create good where I had created evil."

"But you left again."

She rested her face against her tented knees. "Yes, and I can't explain it. I'm not behaving perfectly yet and sometimes it's hard. Even if I can't understand, I've got to believe the end result will be good. I must have done the right thing when I left, because I just had to do it."

He seemed lost in his thoughts. Finally he said, "If you really believe that you can create good in my life, then you're obligated to do so. Come back, Karen, prove your position, and I'll prove mine."

The idea was startling and, as she thought about it, momentarily attractive. She remembered Freddie. "What's the matter?" he asked. "You're trembling."

When she looked up at him, she saw compassion and a deep awareness of her in his eyes. Her throat tightened. She scrambled to her feet and jumped to the ground.

"No, Irish," she said from her safe distance. "There are

some things I thought I could handle when I went back to Denver. Intellectually I know I can handle them, but in reality. . . . " She shook her head and swallowed hard.

Irish was beside her on the ground now and she saw a new concern in his eyes. The expression gave her the renewed desire to prove him wrong and she right. As she looked up at him, she sensed that all this went deeper than the success or failure of a philosophy. It went as deep as life itself. She clenched her hands and stated, "I'm convinced beyond doubt that I'm right. But knowing how stubborn you are, trying to convince you looks like an impossible task."

"How can you object to my staying around for a week or so to present my side of the story?"

She laughed up at him, mockingly, but inside she was trembling. She knew she was being threatened, not by Irish, but by something deep within herself.

The next morning Irish came into the cafe during the breakfast rush. As Karen passed him she noted his fatigue. His face was pale and she saw he walked with a limp. Carrying the platters of ham and eggs and hash browns to the fishermen in the booths, she found herself fretting over the redheaded man who had taken a seat at the counter. As she filled coffee cups and totaled the bills, she kept glancing at the bowed shoulders. When she finally went to the counter she noticed his dejection.

Carrying coffee to him, she watched him glance up as if only then aware of her. "Hi, Karen." He drank the scalding coffee much too fast and she went to cook his breakfast.

Rosemarie watched her flip eggs and add extra ham to the plate. "You kinda' like that guy, pest or not, don't you?"

"I guess he's the type you can't help liking," she said soberly as she picked up the plate. Shoving her way through the swinging doors she had to admit Irish's presence was more disturbing than she wanted it to be.

She hated the reaction she felt when his eyes brightened. "Thanks." He picked up his fork and then watched her clear the counter beside him. The last customer left and Homer went out to the gas pump.

When she brought the coffee pot to the counter she said, "You're tired. I think the mountains don't agree with you."

He grinned at her. "I don't dump that easy."

"Feather bed keep you awake?"

"No, I read most of the night."

"That must have been a real thriller." He didn't answer and she persisted, "Was it?"

"It was the New Testament." Karen couldn't think of anything to say and after a moment, Irish stated, "I needed to be reminded of a few things."

She couldn't help asking, "Like what?"

Homer leaned over the counter. "Karen, take off until dinner time." He looked at Irish. "She hasn't had a real day off since she's been here. Long as you're here, she might as well show you around." Karen didn't like the long appraising look the two men were exchanging.

Homer turned toward her and she slowly removed the apron. "Go get some sandwiches and a thermos of coffee," he ordered. Karen hesitated for a moment and then headed for the kitchen.

The two men watched her walk to the kitchen and then Homer turned. Irish thought Homer's expression was one big question mark, but he only asked, "Need gas?" Nodding, Irish went to move the station wagon to the pumps.

Homer adjusted the hose. As Irish reached for the credit card, he came to lean against the car door. Speaking through the open window Homer said, "She worries me. At nights I hear her crying." He lifted the nozzle and hooked it back on the side of the pump. When he reached for the card his eyes searched Irish's face. "You seem to know her pretty well."

Irish took a deep breath and admitted, "She's my wife. She's having troubles I can't begin to understand and don't know how to reach."

"You a Christian?" Irish nodded and Homer said with satisfaction, "Thought so. It kinda sticks out."

"Look," Irish confided, "she's pretty well shut the door on me. Will you let me know if there's something I should do for her? I've been staying down the road at the Simon's cabins."

Homer nodded and handed the card back. "Sometimes the only thing a body can do is pray. If you believe in God, you've got to believe He can handle the situation better'n you." The gnarled hand with its callouses and grease stains clasped Irish's shoulder and he was comforted.

Chapter 12

When the kitchen door swung closed behind Karen, she went to the refrigerator and Rosemarie said, "Sandwiches? I'll make them. There's the thermos. Use the coffee in here."

Silently, Karen poured coffee. She was feeling as if she were an outsider watching two people she didn't really know. She leaned against the counter and waited for Rosemarie to finish the sandwiches. "Where you two going?" Karen shook her head and plucked at a stubborn hangnail. She was wondering what those two illusionary people would do next. *Would that strange man who was emerging from the shell she called Irish prove to be a man she wouldn't be able to cope with? The strange things he said last night were unsettling, but even more than his words, it was his positive, confident manner that was most unsettling. And Karen, the woman who had spent two years living at a commune, learning how to help people like Irish, was she as impervious to the force to conform as she thought she was?*

She sighed and picked up the lunch. Irish was waiting beside the counter. Reluctantly she moved toward him. He reached for the sack of sandwiches and held the door for her.

Karen was still feeling the separated mood. When he reached inside the station wagon to shove aside the road maps on the seat, she asked, "How's Tina?"

"Fine." His expression was unreadable and that made it easier.

"You two make a good couple, intelligent, sensible," she stopped. Irish was still holding the door and his eyes twinkled with laughter. She felt as if he were seeing something she didn't know existed. Quickly she got into the car and tugged at the door.

After he had slammed his door, he asked, "Who's paying you to be matchmaker? It's certainly not Tina. Karen, you've been trying to get rid of me since the moment I came. That strikes me as sheer panic. Why?"

Karen caught her breath and clenched her fists against her stomach. The teasing expression on his face disappeared and slowly he repeated, "Why?" She watched the play of expression on his face, saw the uncertainty give way to apprehension. Roughly he asked, "Where to?"

"I don't know," she said miserably. "What do you want to see? There's farms and livestock or old mining towns. I don't need to be back until five."

"Let's just wander then. How about taking Highway 84 out of Pagosa Springs?"

They had left Pagosa Springs and were well into the mountains before he spoke again. "Karen, we've got to find a quiet place and talk. Isn't there a picnic area or stream around here?"

"I don't know. This is the first time I've been on this road. I suppose there'll be a dirt road cutting off somewhere." She turned to the window and watched the panorama of pines and mountain peaks with their whipped cream topping of snow. She found herself wishing she was back at the cafe, and idly she wondered where her capacity for enjoying life had disappeared.

There was a dirt road angling away from the highway.

Irish slowed and turned the car. The road was scarcely more than two faint ruts as it left the highway and disappeared in the shallow stream.

As they rocked and bumped over the ruts, Karen saw Irish bite his lip and guessed the pain caused by the motion of the car. "Why don't you just stop here? The car's off the road and that's all that matters." They jolted up out of the stream and he winced. "There, park under that tree," Karen begged.

"I think walking will be a pleasure now." He tried to grin but she saw the white line of pain around his mouth. She found herself wondering again about the suffering he had endured, wondering if it was responsible for the change in him.

He parked the car in the shade of the pine and reached for the thermos and the blanket on the rear seat. She saw the paper-backed Book. "No fair," she protested. "You've brought your Book and didn't tell me to bring mine."

"Oh, but you've been at that meditating business longer than I've been a Christian. By now you should be a master of perfection in the whole affair." She detected the irony. "Come on, let's take our sandwiches and find out where the road goes." He stuffed the Book into his jacket pocket and Karen felt as if she were being backed into a corner.

They followed the old road around a gently rising hill and discovered a mountain meadow dipping toward the distant line of trees.

Gathering clouds purpled the mountain peaks in the distance, but sunshine turned their valley into a spectrum of yellow, green, and blue. "Oh, Irish, look at the flowers. I wish I knew their names. Do you feel like walking farther? See the darling little pink things; they look like miniature elephants."

"Don't step in the water," he cautioned. Karen hopped nimbly across the stream. As they walked through the long grass Irish reached for her arm. When Karen tried to tug away, her feet slipped in the wet grass and he tightened his grip.

He grinned down at her. It was the same light-hearted teasing grin that had been there in the beginning, and Karen's throat ached with the sudden threat of tears. She didn't try to pull away again, but she was painfully aware of the bitter-sweetness of being close to him.

The wind was moving the meadow grass in an undulating sweep, fanning the perfume of marsh and grass and flowers into their faces. When they left the marshy area behind, the road disappeared in a dimming line through the grass. Irish dropped the blanket in a sunny spot. "I think we've about seen the last of that road."

They sat together and ate the sandwiches and drank the coffee. With their shoulders almost touching, they relaxed in the warmth of the sun and for the first time their silence was not uneasy.

Irish reached for her arm. "Look," he whispered, pointing to the trees across the meadow.

A doe stepped into the clearing. She raised her head and looked toward them. Karen guessed from the touch of wind in her face that the doe wouldn't catch their scent.

While they remained motionless two spotted fawns joined the doe and the three moved toward the water pooled at the bottom of the meadow. Karen and Irish watched the deer drink and then graze their way back across to the trees.

When they disappeared into the shadows Karen whispered, "I've never before watched deer like this. Their movements are so smooth they hardly seem real."

Irish nodded and sat up. Unbuttoning his shirt he muttered, "I want to get some sun on my back." Karen reached to help him.

The scar bordering his spine was long and red. "Irish, that's a terrible thing," she said slowly. "And there's another scar near your shoulder blade."

He tried to peer over his shoulder. "I didn't know about that one."

"How could that be? Irish, was it horrible?"

"Not the first ten days." He was laughing at her. "It was only after that there was pain."

"Why?" She folded his shirt and straightened the blanket.

"Well, either I don't remember or I was out of it so I couldn't feel the pain."

She tried to visualize the accident and the days after surgery. She shivered slightly. "I can't begin to understand, but it must have been terrible. To have changed as much as you have would indicate excruciating pain."

He turned to look at her. "Did you see any great difference in me when you first came back to Denver?"

She thought about it for a moment. "No, I really thought you were much the same."

"Then can you understand this? Karen, I told you that I've become a Christian. Is it possible for you to believe that can make a real inward change in a person? Tina was responsible for my seeing a lack in myself. And it wasn't so much what she said but just simply the fact of her life."

There was silence between them as Karen chewed her lip and hunted for words to cut through Irish's strange statements. His convictions were wrong, that she knew, but the undercurrent of feeling in the statements revealed how deeply he was caught up in this emotional experience. She couldn't help studying his face, liking the new gentleness and the aliveness in his eyes, but at the same time, aware of the churning insecurity the discovery was creating in her.

Suddenly he sat up and leaning toward her, he touched her arm. The humble expression on his face was so uncharacteristic of Irish that she forgot to move away. "Karen, I've got to confess something. You're possibly coming back to the worst failure in Denver. I've really gotten myself into a mess. Remember Markham?"

"Yes," she nodded, "and his buddy, what's his name?"

"Norris. Remember I had doubts about him?" She nodded again. "Well, I made a trip to Bloomington's ranch ten days ago and actually stumbled over a drilling core. There's oil on that land and it's out now that Markham intended to develop that land as soon as he could get the contract signed."

"So they were being a little devious. Is it that important?"

"The whole deal is turning out to be a nasty little way of cheating a trusting old farmer by trying to gain his confidence through the use of some dumb young lawyer."

She saw his twisted grin as he tried to say the words lightly. "The duty of this gullible lawyer was to present a bunch of nebulous half promises with an eye to making it all look very candid and open, supposedly an honest bid to buy acreages as a long-term investment. When I finally faced the facts I knew, I realized my job was to use my honest face and a snowstorm of promises to make one man rich at the sacrifice of another's livelihood. That's pretty strong language, but that's just about what it boils down to."

He was silent for a moment before continuing. "I honestly had Bloomington pegged as a sharp old boy. After a few sessions with him I could see he was desperately willing to accept an honest-looking face and promises. In all fairness, I do believe his physical condition had a lot to do with it. He's in constant pain from his arthritis."

"Poor old man. But to think he'd be willing to listen to anything you said, simply because you look honest."

Irish winced. "I'll admit it was my fault from beginning to end. What does it tell you about a guy who allows his head to be turned by a few thousand lousy bucks? Well, you've got it right. When I sat down and really thought about it, I realized I didn't want to be the kind of attorney who makes his living this way."

"They used to call lawyers like that shysters."

"But now they're called shrewd. Karen," he said impatiently, "why is there this blurring of the moral image?" He glanced sharply at her and then continued. "I'm not planning to launch a campaign to alert everyone to the crooked law practices going on in this country, but I did decide I needed to do a little housecleaning on my own premises."

Even as Karen was hearing the words Irish spoke, her mind was busy with the realization that Irish was talking more honestly and intimately than he ever had before. She moved uneasily and wondered where it would all lead. Three years ago this conversation would have filled her with love and hope. She turned away from him.

Irish continued, "You know, I never once questioned Markham and Norris' standing with their company. When I finally got around to asking a few questions I discovered they are neither attorneys nor geologists. They are simply the kind of fellows who have made a living by being Johnny-on-the spot. I have a feeling their past wouldn't bear digging into at all. And I discovered they were more than happy, not only to let me off the hook, but to make the fall easy by padding the ground with a few more green backs. Do you see it, Karen? Your husband has really made a mess of things. Now it'll mean going back to living much as we did in the beginning."

Her mind was flooded with the memories of those early days. There was the picture of the tiny third floor apartment and Irish bounding up the stairs in the evening. Her husband. She squeezed her eyes shut. The momentary threat of warmth and life receded and he seemed to sense it.

Slowly he eased himself back on the blanket and shielded his eyes from the sun. Later, when he began to talk again, it was on a different subject.

"It was Tina who challenged me to read the New Testament."

"All of it?" Karen flipped the pages of the Book, noting the pages that looked as if they had been handled time and time again. She saw places Irish had underlined heavily and other places where he had made notations in the margin.

She felt as if she were handling something deeply intimate. She could almost catch the murmur of a very personal conversation as she studied the underlined words.

In the book of John she saw the words, "The man who puts his faith in him does not come under judgement; but the unbeliever has already been judged in that he has not given his allegiance to God's only Son." The preceding words were underlined too, but the wind caught the pages and ruffled them so Karen went on. In Galatians one section had a box drawn about it and her eyes were drawn to the words: " . . . the life I now live is not my life, but the life which Christ lives in me." She looked at him, wondering if he really believed those words.

"One thing I didn't learn from the reading was the supernatural."

"What do you mean by that? Of course everyone believes God is supernatural."

He went on as if not hearing her. "The Gospels teach that it is necessary to believe that Jesus Christ is God's promised gift, the sin sacrifice. They also got across a point I had missed all along. That is, belief is something that goes down to the very core of a person. It changes you. I couldn't grasp the depth of it all until I read His statements in John. He said if we really believe, we are His friends. Karen, it's a bid for a deeply personal relationship, and you can know you are His friend.

"I just couldn't see how I would live up to the high standards He had set, but I finally gave up and decided I needed to enter this relationship with Christ, even if the attempt to live the life killed me. That's where the supernatural entered in and I didn't grasp it until afterwards.

"It's literally like He told a man named Nicodemus, 'You must be born again.' Faith is a shaky thing until you get your eyes off the things you can see and focus on the spiritual. Then you realize faith is the only unshakeable thing there is.

"I must have faith in God or there is no life. I must have faith in you or there will be no marriage."

Karen felt the deliberate emphasis of his words, and she turned her face away from Irish and buried it in her arms. In the long and absolute silence, he finally touched her shoulder and continued. "When I was able to completely abandon myself to God through believing in Jesus Christ's call to surrender, Karen, I experienced the most unusual thing. There is no way to describe it except to say I now possess Christ, and the other side of the coin is, Christ possesses me. I'm deeply aware of His being, His love and care and even His guidance. It's an inner thing, not an outward trying to live by my own power.

"Karen, you don't need to understand all this to accept Jesus Christ as your own, but you do need to get to the end of your self-sufficiency and have a real desire for Him. No, I guess that isn't right. You must acknowledge the need that's been there all along—it's that universal God hunger."

Now Karen raised her head and saw the yearning love on Irish's face. It tore at her heart but she drawled slowly and deliberately, "You've fallen hook, line, and sinker. You've cast yourself into the palms of an imaginary God and He's going to crush you, squeeze the life out of you. What you call love is really fear. He's got you where He wants you because you'll be afraid to do anything wrong. The fear of God is the beginning of wisdom. Are you wise, Irish? But you are always wise, aren't you? Wise and right. You haven't changed much."

She knew she was not keeping the bitterness out of her voice. Now she had gone beyond being objective, serene. "You're still trying to force your ideas on me in that same overbearing way. Irish has the better idea. Let me tell you," her lips curled with scorn, "I'm not convinced. I like being my own person, thinking my own thoughts, and making up my own mind. I like owning me."

"The typical woman's libber, huh?"

She stopped and thought a moment, "No, I'm not pushing any man down, not even you. It's just that I'm no longer willing to be under your dominance."

"Dominance? Is that your new word for love? If it is, then there isn't any hope, is there?"

"I won't be brain-washed."

"Karen, I'm not trying to push these ideas off as mine. They came from Jesus Christ. I'm only trying to tell you the facts, simply because I can see how deeply you need them."

She snorted with impatience. "You've judged my way without trying it, and yet you expect me to take your word when you push your ideas as better than mine. Let me tell you, Irish," her voice rose, but she didn't care. The frustration was too great. "If you were to have the most convincing argument in the world, which you don't, I wouldn't be willing to accept it or even listen to it, simply because there is nothing in you to show me it is more right than the way I see life.

"You are still saying that it is your goals that are important and valid. I'm saying I've found life much more satisfactory by living it my way with my goals and values. Irish, I wish I could shake some sense into you, you stubborn, hard-headed Irishman. Can't you see? You're not the only right person on this earth. It doesn't matter what you believe. It's how you use what you believe. Even more important than that is my right to believe as I choose."

"Then I guess we've just about come to the end of our road."

"Yes," for a moment her voice was gentle. "I'm rather sorry, but my real regret is that I can't somehow give you the impetus to try meditation. It is the most fantastic—"

Abruptly she jumped to her feet and danced a lighthearted step away from him. "Darling, Irish, you pushed the burden of your religion on me; now I'll tell you. Come out of it. There must be progress. Hurry on with me and see what I have to bring you. Life is evolving, changing, and everyone in this world must be pressed into the purpose of helping life evolve higher and higher. See, now we're all caught in this tangled web of hate and fear, war and pollution and," she stopped for breath.

Irish rolled over on the blanket and buried his face in his arms. She knelt beside him. Goaded by a nameless something she said, "You wanted me back." She caught her breath and trembled. She was glad he couldn't see her face. Carefully she took a deep breath and said, "Okay. You want me back and I'll come to Denver with you if you'll forget this nonsense and let me help you learn real peace through meditation."

He rolled over and looked up into her face. She steeled herself to remain motionless, to stay close to him no matter what he might do. Suddenly he began to laugh. It was mirthless and mocking. She rocked back on her heels and asked, "What's so funny?"

"Do you know why I came?" He sat up and carefully moved himself around to face her. "I gave up Tina because He, Christ, let me see through God's Word just how wrong divorce is. Paul very carefully points out in his letters that the position of a Christian man is to create a pattern of love for his wife in much the same way Christ loves His church. The church, for your information, is all those believers who are truly committed to Him. See, being a Christian demands of me total obedience to Christ, total commitment to Him. Being a Christian demands I claim my wife and have a Christ-centered home."

"Very flattering," she mocked. "If I'd any illusion of love, you've set me straight. The knight in shining armor pursues his lady, not because of love but because God makes him."

The old teasing expression was back in Irish's eyes and he laughed. Unexpectedly he bent over her. "Jealous? Let me prove otherwise." She moved away and the expression faded.

With a sober intensity that caught Karen off guard and convinced her where she didn't think it was possible to be convinced, he said, "Karen, I couldn't come after you until God changed me. I really hated you for walking out on me without even telling me why. It was the most traumatic experience I've ever endured, and I was absolutely positive I couldn't love you again. You see, for two years this feeling was deep enough that, for me, you ceased to exist. I didn't want you back. I didn't want to face the hurts you caused and learn to live with them. It just didn't seem worth it. I'd found Tina and I wanted her, so much so that I was willing to pursue her ideas of God. But when God became a reality to me and I was willing to accept Him as Savior, then I realized the first thing I had to do to get God's forgiveness was to forgive you for what you'd done to me."

He paused and took a deep breath. "That was completely impossible. That is, all on my own it was. I tried in every way I could to forgive you, to resolve the whole mess of my feelings toward you, but I couldn't do it until I asked Christ to handle it for me.

"Karen, it was like rolling up a bunch of dirty laundry and pitching it at Him. Don't ask me how an emotion can be changed, because I can't give you an answer. I do know I was absolutely wrung out and exhausted from the emotional upheaval. Then I experienced a sense of deep and total peace and the knowledge that I love you more now than I ever have before."

Karen smoothed the nap of the blanket, traced its plaid with a trembling finger and wondered what to say. Momentarily she faced that black burden between them and wondered how unshakeable Irish's peace and love would be if she were to tell him about it.

The moment passed and Irish was talking again. "Now you're saying you'll come back as my wife if I give up my relationship to Christ." She started to protest but he interrupted, "Karen, be honest, that's the essence of your request. Think. Your meditating demands a focus and it isn't on what Christ has done for you, but instead on what you can do for yourself. Do you realize the whole thrust of the New Testament deals with this idea? Jesus told the Jews over and over again to quit trying to be religious, to quit trying to earn their righteousness by following their rule book. Now the modern thing, you tell me, is to go back to the same old rut of trying to drag yourself up to God's level by your own effort."

"But your daddy-son relationship is all wrong," Karen cried. "That's a juvenile picture that went out with the ark."

Surprise showed on his face. "Why do you say that? Karen, even Jesus Christ's prayer started, 'Our Father.' If there's a failure, perhaps it's because our view of the Father is all wrong."

"Oh, no, that's not it. My father knew he was god and he never let me forget it."

His expression became thoughtful as he reached for her hand. "Karen, you've never talked about your father very much. I know he didn't have much to do with raising you because you've talked so much about your governess, Mrs. Ormand. What was your father like?"

Karen had no intention of dragging out the old pictures, but the gentleness of Irish's voice and the tender tugging on her hand seemed to force the words. "When I was a little girl," she began dully, "I had a beautiful doll. Daddy brought her back from France. Her hair was long and black and piled on her head in a mass of curls. Her dress was silk, white with embroidered roses. Irish, she had jeweled earrings and velvet slippers too." Unconsciously Karen had clasped her hands to her stomach. Irish reached to pull them back to him.

She couldn't keep the tremor out of her voice, "But I couldn't play with her. She sat on the bookcase in my father's library. I could only look. While he was gone one afternoon I gave in to temptation and got her down." She looked at him. "You must understand, I wasn't being careless, but the only way I could reach her was by stacking the foot stool in the rocking chair." She pulled her hand away from his and wrapped her arms around her tented knees.

"The rocker slipped and the doll was absolutely smashed to bits. I spent the rest of the afternoon there in that dark, cold room and when he came home there was thunder and lightning and Karen went up to her room in the dark."

Suddenly Karen straightened and said, "I don't know why I told you that. I hadn't even thought of the incident for ages, and I've presented all the wrong view of him. I guess I shouldn't have been given that doll in the first place. I wasn't up to the responsibility of it. But," she found the words bursting from her unwilling lips, "why must I be punished forever? It isn't right, is it?" She caught her breath in a gasp.

Irish's brow furrowed into heavy lines. He rubbed his hands over his face, dropped them and slowly said, "Karen, what do you mean? Can't you forgive yourself for breaking the doll? I'm certain your father has long ago forgotten the incident."

Karen laughed and pressed a shaky hand against her face. "It's all just a silly, little-girl feeling. Besides, guilt is gross; therefore it doesn't exist."

"I'll bet," Irish said, "there's a million people in this world who would like to believe that."

She leaned forward, "And that's my mission—to tell them all that very thing."

She got to her feet. "Well, we'd better run now or I'll be late for work." She held his shirt for him, eased it over his sunburned shoulders. "You'll need lotion on your back."

In silence they drove back to the cafe. It wasn't an easy silence now. Karen was aware of all the heavy, unanswerable questions hanging between them. She still wondered about his bitter reaction to her proposal and wondered also

182

why she couldn't touch him without experiencing the strange, fearful, churning sensation.

They were almost to the cafe when he spoke. "Karen, I want you back, but your terms are wrong and I can't accept them. I'm convinced Christianity is the only right way to live."

Her gesture was tired and impatient. "Right? All religions are right. You can't judge meditation until you've tried it."

"I've told you about the experience I've had with Christ. I'm completely confident of my position in Christ. One thing I am certain about is that, for me, guilt is a very real thing. I no longer have a sense of guilt over my past. This is based on my willingness to believe in what Jesus Christ has done for me. Does meditation do that for you?"

"Guilt?" she said hastily. "I've told you, that's only something experienced on the gross level of life, the animal level. On the spiritual level there's no such thing; I have no guilt." She spoke confidently, but she was uneasily aware of the sleepless nights, with that gnawing, empty feeling in her stomach.

They were pulling into the parking lot at the cafe when Irish spoke, and the tone of his voice made Karen look at him. "Just before I left Denver, Freddie called. She asked about you."

Did she sense a hidden question in his voice? She studied his face, saw the white line around his mouth, but couldn't guess the expression his sun glasses shielded. Uneasily she moved her shoulders against the seat back.

Still conversationally he asked, "Do you miss the studio and the rest of them?"

"No," she shook her head to hide the shiver of distaste. "Never."

"I suppose Freddie was a hard person to work with."

"You didn't seem to think that at the time you arranged the job for me." Karen knew there was a challenge in her voice and when he faced her briefly she said, "Freddie swallows people whole."

"Why did you say that?"

Feeling as if she had stepped on marshy ground, she said slowly, "You think and feel and act like Freddie if you want to get along with her. You must be a little Freddie, not a big one. Oh dear," she mocked, "never that."

She paused and then asked, "Do you mind driving me up to the house? I'm a little late and I must change."

For a moment Irish's hands rested against the steering wheel. He was watching Karen's face, noting how the deeply shadowed eyes seemed to veil her feelings. Sighing with frustration, he guided the car through the trees and parked beneath the drooping branches of a blue spruce.

In the two days he had been with Karen the nagging questions had been growing. It was now or never. "Karen," he paused long enough to take a deep breath. "When I talked to Freddie she asked me if I knew about the baby. Karen, do we have a baby?"

It was like watching flesh turn to stone. White alabaster. The alabaster hand rigid on the door handle jerked. "No." The white face was a hard mask. A hidden corner of his thoughts reminded him that he had been warned. She pushed the door open and stepped to the ground. Almost he expected her to leave without saying more.

Abruptly she circled the car and leaned on his door. The mask was still there and her eyes glittered. "Remember, Irish? You said God made you love me more than ever before. I can prove that's an illusion. Dan," now she was mocking Tina's gentle voice, "Dan St Clair, I killed your baby."

"What?" He thrust the door open and the force threw Karen to the ground. Standing over her, he shouted, "You did what to my baby?"

She raised to one elbow. "Remember, you said no kids.

Well, I just followed orders. No kids. I had an abortion."

Leaning over her, he jerked her to her feet. "Tell me that's a lie, just another way to hurt me."

"No, Irish." Now her voice was rising; tears glittered on the white mask. "I killed your baby. You made me do it. Me, the dutiful wife, tearing the life out to give you what you wanted. Only this time it didn't work. I tore my soul out too. Irish, I'll hate you until I die."

Her voice dropped to a whisper. "Can you imagine the torment? Night after night I've awakened, thinking I hear that baby cry. Every child I see accuses me for what I've done. That's what I live with. That's what I'm doomed to live with for the rest of my life."

He was remembering the brief he had prepared for Jeff Evin. Slowly he said, "At conception there is life. At no time from the moment of union is that embryo less than a human being capable of feeling and response. A tiny creation in God's likeness."

He realized he was squeezing Karen's shoulders, and that her gasps were of pain. Abruptly he released her and walked away.

He didn't know where he walked or for how long. Suddenly it was dark and he was sitting on the steps of his cabin. He became conscious of the evening chill through his thin shirt; his sunburned flesh quivered in response. When strength and reason returned, he realized there was only one thing he wanted.

Heaving himself off the steps, he moved stiff muscles and stumbled into the cabin. Yanking down the suitcase he began cramming clothing into it. When he realized the wads were resisting his careless hands, he slowly sat down and tried to fold them into acceptable shapes. He concentrated on breathing deeply as he worked. Trying to move back into the sphere of rational thinking and action, he looked around the room. A bitter smile twisted his lips when he saw the colorful patchwork quilt.

Yesterday afternoon, when he had rented this cabin, he had been full of bright, foolish dreams. Dreams of bringing Karen here to stay. A sweet Karen in his arms again, his wife again. He rubbed at the sick, cold perspiration on his forehead and tried to forget her.

Was it only a week ago that his thought had been full of Tina and the agony of having to surrender her? Despite the fact he thought of her without desire, he found himself wondering if the situation had changed. Would God condemn him for having Tina after what Karen had done?

He mulled over the commitment he had made the previous week. The agony of his inability to forgive Karen had been real. His thoughts moved on to the next step. Without a doubt, being able to forgive Karen had been a divine gift, and God was fully aware of what she had done. Where did that leave him now?

He pulled the suitcase to the floor and cautiously lowered himself. Face down across the bed, his thoughts wandered back to the afternoon he and Karen had spent together. Until their conversation he hadn't tried to put into words all that had taken place in his life. Now he was realizing that, strangely enough, trying to explain all that had happened had cemented that decision and helped him realize the supernatural turning his life had taken. After having made the hard decision to let Jesus Christ direct his life, would he back down now?

After a long time he could address that person. "Okay, Lord, I'm not backing down. I'm still just reeling from the shock of this. Doesn't what Karen's done change everything?"

He was caught up in the comparison of sins. There was no doubt of the lesser and greater. Then he remembered. In the soul searching he had done before making that final commitment to Christ, he had realized his greatest sin was refusing to accept the completed atonement. What was Karen's sin in comparison to that rejection? Abruptly he was filled with the yearning desire to see the pain and fear erased from Karen's face.

There was something in the Bible that was nagging at his thoughts. He wanted to read it. Sitting up he flipped on the light. It was Ephesians 5:25 and he muttered the key words, "Husbands, love as Christ loved and gave."

He lay face down again. For a long, silent time he was full of rebellion. Finally, he groaned agonizingly, "But it was my child."

Now he remembered something he had heard as a boy. He felt again the horror he had experienced then. It was in church. The preacher had leaned far out over the pulpit and wagging a long bony finger that seemed to point right at Irish, he had said, "Don't you blame the Jews for killing Jesus. You killed God's Son. It was your sins that killed Him just as surely as if you'd been the only sinner in the whole world."

Irish sighed. The hurt was still bitter and fresh. "Okay, Lord. My hurt is not greater. My sin no less. I forgive."

Chapter 13

Irish could hear a vehicle. The noise of its engine penetrated his uneasy sleep and became louder before it stopped. Irish sat up and peered at his watch. Its hands pointed to one-thirty. Shaking it he got up and went to the door.

"Homer. Is something wrong?"

"I thought this is something you'd better know about." Homer was breathless. "You're her husband."

"What is it?" he questioned, buttoning his jacket.

"Heard her crying again and then she got up and went out. I got dressed. Figured I'd go talk to her for a little bit, but before I could get to her, she left in that little bug. She's headed up the road and it ends at the old log bridge. There's nothing above it except for the old mining town. If she goes up there in the dark, she could get hurt. There's lots of these old mining shafts around that aren't too well covered. If she steps—" he stopped and Irish came through the door.

"I'll drive. I brought your station wagon back to you, and I know the road better'n you." Homer led the way.

When they reached the creek, Irish saw the Volkswagen with its front wheels in the water. "There's her car. Looks almost like she tried to ford the stream."

Irish was out of the station wagon almost before it stopped. He hesitated on the bank, wishing he had worn his back brace. The logs were too risky in the dark. He took a deep breath and plunged into the icy water.

He could hear Homer laboring up the slope behind him, but he didn't slow down. As Irish climbed he was filled with a sense of foreboding. Perhaps it was just the lonely mountainside and the darkness that accounted for his mood. But he couldn't help remembering Karen's stony white face. Now, with a sense of shock, he could accept the fact that to him what Karen had done was no longer as important as who she was. Now he wondered if he would be able to transcend all those bitter events to reach her. For a moment his legs were lead and he had to force them to move up that hill.

When Irish reached the first group of buildings, the moon broke through the drifting clouds and touched the slanting roofs with reflected silver. He stood on the long abandoned road and turned slowly. Wind rattled a weathered board and banged it against its companion. The hollow plop echoed through the empty building, and re-echoed through his mind, reinforcing the loneliness.

Irish waited, listening. He sensed the loneliness was more than a mood. It was as real as a person. Could that person be Karen? He was glad for the crunch of Homer's boots on the cindered path.

"Seems I heard a rock roll." Homer's voice was hushed. "It'd be up the slope on the far end of town." They followed the dim path of the old road.

When Irish started to cut across a pile of tumbled timbers, Homer took his arm. "There could be a shaft under that pile. Best stick to the road."

The creek trickled across in front of them, spilling away from the old mill and settling ponds. Again Irish paused to listen for movement. The wind whipped his damp clothes and he shivered.

"We're almost to the end of it," Homer advised him. "The road ends just on the other side of these buildings. I wouldn't expect to find her here anyway. She's probably climbed the rocks at the end of the road. There's a purty view from them, but in the dark they're tricky. Let's head up there." They waded through the stream, this time wetting only their shoe soles.

At the end of the road the cliff reared in front of them as abruptly as a wall. Its mounding base was covered with scrub pine and sage brush, but higher up Irish could see the cluster of bare rock, rising against the sky like leaning dominoes.

A shadowy movement caught his eyes. He stood motionless straining to see. Again the movement, and now Homer saw it too. "She wouldn't jump, would she?" Homer's words were slow and doubtful. Irish shook his head, unable to force his voice past the tightness in his throat. But could he deny the possibility?

When Irish could talk he murmured, "I don't think she knows anyone is around. We could startle her by shouting. I'm going to try to follow her up."

The shadow seemed to settle against the lower section of rocks. "Go around that way," Homer pointed, "where she won't be as likely to see you."

Irish nodded and whispered, "Would you—?" He couldn't finish.

Homer touched his arm and nodded. "I'll go back down that way, just in case. Now you cut back aways. It's easier going." He moved off through the shadows.

Quietly Irish moved toward the base of the cliff. The darkness lay against his face like a muffling hand, and he had to strain around it. There was the trail and he was grateful for its smoothness. He climbed swiftly and silently.

Just ahead he could see her sitting on a rock, silhouetted against the sky. As Irish quietly moved toward her in the moonlight, he could see the glitter of tears on her face. He tried to control his steps, but tension tightened his muscles and a rock slipped. She turned and saw him.

Like a wild thing moving toward the safety of the shadows, she slipped from her perch and climbed higher up the sloping rocks. He could hear loose stones tumbling and bumping. Then, after a silence, he heard a crashing far below.

He caught his breath and momentarily was gripped by fear of the dark and unknown. He waited, listening, trying to determine her movements. In the stillness there was only the keening of the wind through the trees and rocks.

Now, from across the valley, came the cry of a coyote. As the sound bounced off the hills, he whispered, "Karen." Now louder, "Karen, it's me, Irish." In the silence he realized she was running, not from the unknown, but from him. Again he saw her before she turned and disappeared.

He started up the last slope, working his way around the edge of the cliff. He dared not look back over his shoulder, knowing there was only black shadow below. Realizing every movement must be carefully made, both for his safety and Karen's too, he crawled through loose gravel, grasping trees and bushes and then reaching again. Finally he rounded the treacherous point and could breathe easier again.

When she was outlined against the sky with no higher rock remaining, he paused. His muscles were trembling with strain, and he dared not attempt that last slope that separated them. The white of her tennis shoe gleamed just beyond his hand. He wanted more than anything to lunge at that shoe, but he folded his arms on the chest-high rock and tried to calm his heavy breathing.

Her voice was remote, emotionless, in harmony with the end-of-the-world spot she had chosen. "I just wanted to be alone." The wind swirled her dark curls into a halo around her face, making her eyes brilliant against the paleness of her skin. The wind kicked dust into his face and he rubbed his eyes, blinking up at her.

There seemed to be an even deeper quietness about her. He sensed an air of resignation that stabbed him with fear. He couldn't forget those last words she had said the afternoon before. Could he admit the possibility of that thing Homer hinted?

He kept his voice low, hoping to entice her to move closer. "Karen." If only he dared close that gap and grasp that foot. But the gap wasn't only physical. He fought for words to bridge the gulf.

"Karen." What words do you choose when a person is a step away from that black void? "Karen, I still mean it. I love you."

Her white face was pointed toward him now and her back to the moonlight.

"Now I must ask. Karen, will you please forgive me?" Curiosity brought her nearer and his fingers tightened on the rock.

"Forgive you?" She spoke as if her lips were stiff. "Why?"

"Because the ultimate responsibility is mine. Karen, I want with all my heart to see you come to God. I want to see the heartache gone and I want my Karen back. Only I want her to become a new Karen, new in Christ."

"You still want to control and change, don't you?" Her voice was a bitter whisper. Irish's patience snapped and he lunged. The loose rock beneath his feet slipped and he fell, slipping and rolling through rocks and bushes. Even as he fought to control his fall, he welcomed the gouging rocks as a purge from the deeper pain. Abruptly he slid face first into a clump of sagebrush.

Slowly he sat up. He felt the sore spots and cautiously moved his shoulders. Karen slid down beside him. Her voice was still and remote. "Are you hurt?"

"Only a few scrapes."

She moved closer and in a quick movement, he grabbed her arm and pulled her down beside him. Through clenched teeth he said, "You're getting down this mountain in one

192

piece, even if I have to knock you out to get you there."

While he was taking a deep breath she said, coldly, "Don't be ridiculous. I have no intention of getting down in any other condition."

He tried to break through the wall. "Karen, why can't you act like a living, moving, breathing human being? Doesn't anything touch you anymore?" She was shaking her head and pulling away from his hand. "Talk to me," he pleaded.

Now she whispered, "Can't you understand? This is God's judgment. I'm frozen inside and I can never be your wife again. The past is bad karma and there's no going back. I can only go on and it must be alone." He felt as if she were using the words like knives to cut chasms between them.

Her voice was without emotion as she continued. "Until that terrible thing happened I never realized there was a God watching me, knowing everything I did. I'll never live on the gross level again."

Irish remembered the way she had reacted when he tried to kiss her. The shrinking horror in her eyes should have warned him.

She was speaking again and, from the dream-like quality of her words, he wondered if she really understood all that she was saying. "Even in the beginning, they are complete little humans. A tiny, trusting infant, and I offered only death. From the first I blamed you for everything. I hated you for forcing on me the necessity of that step. I hated and hated. Now," her voice broke and then took on a new bleakness, "I realize the guilt is truly mine. I can no longer escape it."

"Karen, I take your guilt. I accept responsibility for what happened. I will be the guilty one." She turned to look at him and wide-eyed she moved closer, studying his face as if trying to see deep into him. He took her arm gently, "Would you be able to believe in God's forgiveness if that terrible guilt weren't there?"

Moving as if awakening, she stirred and replied slowly, "Yes, of course. Then I wouldn't be so evil." Again the silence and then, "But the guilt is there. I can't escape it."

"Jesus said He didn't come to judge our sins but to save us from them. He showed me the worst sin I had was rejecting Him."

He could see she wasn't listening. She was saying, "The guilt isn't transferable like bonds. Someday, perhaps, I'll be able to live above it."

"By meditating and pretending it doesn't exist? Karen, I wish I could convince you. Jesus Christ can forgive what you are fighting to ignore." Now in the moonlight he could see her face was flat, finally and completely closed to him. He knew there was nothing else to be said. Her rejection was final and total. His back was throbbing with the bruising it had taken.

He stood up and pulled her to her feet. "Let's get off the mountain."

She pulled away and made her last statement. "Your way takes faith. Gramps told me that means believing God means what He says." She shivered. "I could find no way to believe in that kind of forgiveness, even if I dared ask."

Wearily he watched her, feeling the gulf between them widen. He remembered the story of the broken doll and his tired mind juggled the parallel. But a broken doll was insignificant to the pain she was experiencing now. Yet she had cried in rebellion against the lack of forgiveness she sensed in that incident.

A stone rolled and Irish looked up. Homer pulled himself up to their level. "Everything okay?" he asked.

Irish saw the kindly face was creased with weariness and some of the pain around his own heart eased. Silently he gave Karen to Christ again. "Not all right yet," he said slowly, "but it's all in good hands."

Karen looked from Homer to Irish. Her shoulders drooped and she poked the gravel with her foot. "I'm sorry," she whispered. "I can't quite understand this all. I just wanted to be by myself." Her head came up in defiance and she straightened her shoulders. "But, I've inconvenienced you. I'm terribly sorry."

The old Karen, Irish thought, *back in her shell. What all has she had to go through behind that wall she's built around herself?*

Silently they walked down the slope and back through the empty street. The silvered boards and creaking doors reminded Irish that life was past for the people who had lived here. As their heels had crunched the cinders and then moved on, now Irish and Karen too were moving, crunching across the same cinders. He couldn't help wondering if their passing would be as futile and empty with dead dreams.

Silently they crossed the stream and Homer got into the Volkswagen with Karen. Irish closed her door, realizing the full significance of that act.

He leaned over to see her dark eyes in the moonlight. "There isn't anything else I can do, is there?"

Her lips trembled, tightened. She shook her head. "No," it was a whisper. "This is best. Please leave me now, Irish. It's finished."

When he was in the feather bed, sleepless and tense, he forced stiff lips to say, "It's your burden, Jesus Christ. There's nothing I can do now."

In the morning he knew it was time to return to Denver.

When he walked into the restaurant, only Rosemarie was there. He slid onto a stool, picked up the menu and asked, "Where's Karen?"

"I don't know," she glared at him as if she held him responsible.

Karen still hadn't come by the time he finished breakfast. He paid his bill and said, "Tell Karen I've gone back to Denver. She knows how to contact me." He made his grin carefree and jaunty, but underneath it he was admitting that Karen wouldn't be back.

He turned the station wagon toward Pagosa Springs. As

he drove into the mountains he found himself praying desperately. And when he wasn't praying, his thoughts filled with the memory of Karen's unhappy face. Even as he berated himself for leaving her in such a state, he was gently urged into the realization that the situation wasn't his concern now.

He was into the mountains. Climbing toward Wolf Creek Pass, he realized the switchbacks were beginning to make his back ache. He shifted his position and admitted he should have worn his back brace. He shifted again and tried to relax into the movement of the vehicle. The panorama of trees and mountain peaks unrolled before him and he tried to appreciate the view, but the pain grew.

Finally, miserably aware of only his discomfort, he pulled into a roadside parking area. Getting out of the car he moved around, trying to work the stiffness and pain out of his body.

Just over the edge of the road and down a few steps from the graveled area where he stood was a large flat rock. It sloped gently into the sunlight. He eased himself down over the edge and crawled onto the rock. As he had guessed, the rock was hot from the heat of the sun and he gratefully stretched out.

Chapter 14

The tears were rolling down Karen's face and dropping on her folded hands. Gramps sat across the table from her, hunched over the black Book. There were traces of moisture glittering in that white halo of hair and Karen was still astonished at the way she had cried all over him and then told him the whole story. It hadn't been easy to admit the spiraling disintegration of their marriage with its culmination, the abortion.

She sighed and rubbed her aching forehead. "We've talked and talked. I guess confession is supposed to be good, but I don't feel any better, I don't think."

He glanced up and there was a measure of sternness in his light blue eyes. "When you get away from the things it says about God in the Book, then your whole view of God is distorted. You can't expect a few words to erase all the stuff you've been puttin' into your mind. You're going to have to do a little re-educatin'. The whole trouble is you didn't have a good picture of God before you got yourself into this mess."

Karen dropped her head and he continued, "Now listen. John 3:16 tells us that God loved us all so much He gave His Son so that we could have life, and over here in Isaiah it tells how. Way before Jesus was born, God told us what He intended to do. And it's true." He paused and peered over the top of his spectacles. His fingers fumbled with the pages.

"It's like He couldn't hardly wait until that time He would send His Son, and He had to tell about it in advance. There. Isaiah 53:4, 'Surely he hath borne our griefs and carried our sorrows,' and 'He was wounded for our transgressions, he was bruised for our iniquities: the chastisement of our peace was upon him; and with his stripes we are healed . . . the Lord hath laid on him the iniquity of us all.' "

Karen asked, "Are you trying to say God will forgive even all that I've told you? Sure it all sounds wonderful. But that kind of a God is so remote. I can't connect all those beautiful words with my life—there's just no reality to it." Moving her shoulders restlessly, she leaned across the table and said, "All this still doesn't tell me why, all night long, I kept hearing Irish saying over and over that he would be the guilty one. It was horrible." She bit her lip. "I know he can't. That's all ridiculous. Guilt isn't transferable. But I can't get away from those words. Why?"

Gramps folded his hands on the Bible and said slowly, "Well, it seems to me that the fella was just putting into words what the Bible tells him to do. Over in Ephesians it says a man's supposed to love his wife just the way Jesus loved the church and gave himself for it." He peered at her. "Do you understand?"

"I don't understand anything except the terrible expression on Irish's face when he said that," Karen whispered. "He looked as if he was living that horrible, sick guilt. The same guilt I felt."

"You mean he never did approve of what you did?"

"Oh, Gramps," Karen touched her face with a trembling hand, "when I told him, I thought he would kill me. Just for a moment."

Gramps jabbed at a faded flower on the oilcloth. "I guess," he muttered, "that's just about as close an illustration as you could get to the real atonement."

Wearily Karen rested her head on her folded arms. She felt as if she were being lifted out of her misery and being allowed to see a picture suddenly brought into sharp focus. "But I don't understand it."

Gramps said, "If you believe Jesus Christ really was God, like the Bible says, and that He willingly became a man, lived and died just like any other man, well then—"

Karen knew her husky voice was almost inaudible, but it was all right. She spoke for herself. "You're saying He must have looked much like Irish did. His face must have reflected the horror of all those terrible things He was seeing and hearing. Only when Irish said he would be guilty, he didn't have to die for the guilt."

"You mean," Gramps asked, "that the whole idea of God is still pretty fuzzy? But that if you could see in Irish what God did—"

Karen stood up. "I do see. At least I think I'm beginning to see. If I can just really think about it. If I concentrate hard enough on the love and forgiveness I saw in Irish's face, then maybe I'll be able to believe some day that God could feel that way about me." She took a deep breath of relief.

"You know, Irish tried to tell me these things and all I could see was that he was trying to push his ideas off on me again in that overbearing, pigheaded way." Unconsciously her hands clenched just thinking about his habit of force that she remembered from the past.

"Now the whole thing not only makes sense to me, but it's like watching the pattern of forgiveness being acted out in front of me. I can't deny the suffering I saw in his face." Her voice broke, she swallowed hastily and asked, "Gramps, is it possible to love someone when you think you are really hating?"

Gramps looked bewildered for a second and then replied slowly, "I 'spect so. But it seems to me that loving is something you make up your mind to do and just do it—that is, you let God do it in you. Love is from God, a gift. Now hate, well, that's a kind of sick thing that doesn't belong in a well person at all. I sure don't think you can ever get rid of that by making up your mind to it. I have an idea that it would leave a hole that's got to be filled with something, and if it isn't love, well, I suppose the hate would come back stronger than ever."

Karen chewed the tip of her finger for a moment and then said, "Now I take it you're telling me I've got to decide whether I will be sick or well, aren't you?"

She could see the twinkle come back into Gramps' eyes and she slowly got to her feet. "I give up."

"What's that?" She looked at Gramps' puzzled face.

"This mess that's been going on inside. I'm being pulled to pieces. I don't know why but meditation is all wrong. It's like something has a stranglehold on me and every time I say that word, I'm less capable of being my own person. Now, since I've been around here, I've felt as if I'm a battleground. I can't take anymore." Her voice shook and she swallowed hard before continuing. "I'll never meditate again. I've got to get away from that feeling. I give up."

She stepped around the table and rested her hand on Gramps' shoulder. "I've got to talk to Irish. It's awfully important now that I say I'm sorry to him."

Rosemarie greeted her blandly as she walked in the door, "I thought you were supposed to be here for the breakfast rush."

Karen blinked. She tried to bring her thoughts to the present. "I'm sorry. I overslept," she said slowly. "And then Gramps and I talked. He's, well, he's so wise."

Rosemarie snorted. She filled a glass with water and thumped it on the counter. "Is that more important than being over here? Your young man said to tell you he's heading back to Denver."

"Irish. You mean Irish has gone?" She licked dry lips. "When?"

"An hour or so ago. Isn't that what you wanted?"

Letty came into the cafe carrying Amy. Karen hurried toward her. "Letty, Irish has left and I must see him." Letty nodded wisely. Karen hesitated. Touching Amy's hand she was filled with shame for the times she had rebuffed her baby advances. Leaning forward she pressed her lips to the child's soft neck. "Sweet, darling baby," she whispered and then was out the door.

The Volkswagen sluggishly came to life. Despite her best efforts, Karen could only coax the vehicle into a lethargic fifty miles an hour.

She settled back and tried to make her tense body relax, to accept the discipline of a long, hard drive. She wished she dared ask God to help her find Irish. She felt her body slipping toward the remembered limpness of meditation, and she deliberately shoved her mind back into sharp, thinking focus. "Oh, no you don't. That's over for good."

She concentrated on reviewing the surprising things that had been happening to her. The long night hours had been a constant revelation as she tossed on her bed. Now for the first time in her life she was standing before an open door. But where did the door lead, and why was she hesitating on the threshold?

Karen tried to sort through the experiences that led to that feeling. Was it possible that just admitting her guilt could bring relief? And could that relief give the assurance that life was really unfolding with promise and meaning now that she had taken the right step for once?

She must find Irish. There was a strange feeling being generated, and it convinced her that the first step toward freedom involved finding him.

The afternoon shadows were deepening into blue purple

against the base of the mountains as she headed up the highway toward Wolf Creek Pass.

Her whole attention was fastened on the road in front of her. She felt as if it were her strength alone willing the car up the slope. Without a doubt she wouldn't catch up with Irish, but she was determined to drive until she reached Denver.

She almost missed the station wagon. As she flashed past the roadside park, she caught a glimpse of the blue nose sticking out through the trees. At the first straight stretch, she whipped the Volkswagen around and headed back.

It was his car. She recognized the blanket, the paperback New Testament, and even the old familiar suitcase; but the door hung open and he was nowhere to be seen.

She listened and in the mountain quiet there was only the passing of a vehicle and the sound of the wind in the trees. Turning to the station wagon again, she noticed that the ignition key was still in place.

While she looked at the key, fearful mental images began to crowd through her mind. She tried to push away the clinging thought that grasped at her mind telling her that she was too late, that she was doomed forever by a karma she couldn't control.

She pressed trembling hands to her face and tried to think constructively, with that part of her mind that could reason and think and act. She would need to get help. The wind moved the bushes skirting the edge of the parking lot. Could he have fallen?

She climbed over the guard rail and looked down the rocky slope. The mountainside was dangerously steep. Again the wind moved bushes and swirled dust. As she bowed her head to the dust, she caught a flash of red through the bushes.

Irish had a red shirt. She grasped the bush in front of her and eased herself forward. To her left, on a flat boulder only a few yards from the road, she could see Irish. He was lying sprawled, his head turned away from her. In a curiously lifeless way the wind lifted his red hair and ruffled it across his forehead.

He had fallen. Karma. It was true. Those insidious fingers were real. For a moment she stood looking down at the rock, paralyzed by all that had happened. But now there was a new something. She took a deep breath and discovered she could think, remember. Last night when he had fallen and rolled down that slope, she had watched with the curious detachment of a bystander only remotely interested. Now, with his body crumpled on the rocks below, alarm surged through her body. This was her husband and she would not let him die.

Moving from one boulder to another she scrambled down the steep slope. Cutting across now, she dropped onto the rock and crawled toward him. She could see his arms were limp and turned in an awkward way. As she approached his eyes opened and he watched without moving.

She rocked back on her heels, moistened her lips and whispered, "Did you fall?"

"No." He waited and she could see the hurt deep in his eyes. All of the passion—that high resolve that had sent her after him—had faded and she settled numbly communing with the hurt. His voice was flat, expressionless, as he asked, "Why have you come?"

She stirred, tried to move her eyes from his and attempt the light-hearted touch. "I . . . I guess I've got my thumb out again."

Moving stiffly, he shoved himself into a sitting position and faced her. "Didn't we decide that was impossible?"

"Irish." The words wanted to come in a rush now. She clenched her hands in her lap and steeled herself to break through that cold curtain around him. "I'm here to say I'm sorry. Can you see what that means?"

"I'm not certain."

"It was something big for me to be able to face what I've done. I've quit blaming you and I can accept that horrible, sick guilt because for the first time since it's happened there's hope. Gramps told me this morning that when God forgives sin, in His eyes that sin ceases to exist. You'll never know how badly I've wished for something like that to happen every day of the past two years." Tears scalded her cheeks and her clenched hands, but through her swimming vision she saw the heavy lines on Irish's face begin to relax.

Her voice dropped to a whisper. "It's impossible to live close to a person holding that horrible, guilty secret. That's why I had to leave."

"But you wouldn't have done it in the first place if your marriage had been good and whole. My failure really does make me a party to your sin."

"Do you, could you—" Her lips were too stiff to form the words.

"Yes, I can accept you without ever bringing this up again. You see, Karen, I must. That's the workable part of forgiveness."

"Then may I—" Again she couldn't finish the sentence, but while the tears trickled down her cheeks, she lifted her hitchhiking thumb. He looked at it and then covered her hand with his own.

"One thing I've learned—I guess God has been hammering it into my hard head—is the supreme value of the total human—body, soul, and mind. Karen, will you take me back? May I be your husband again?"

She looked past the tears in his eyes, the lines on his face, and saw the comfort and promise waiting for her. She held out her arms and wordlessly they clung, healing the fracture and sharing the comfort.

He finally freed a hand and pushed her head back to see her eyes. "Karen, we've failed before. Don't you see? We'll fail again unless we have something more?"

She nodded. "All along I sensed a need and a promise of

something more in our marriage. There was a hint of an elusive richness that made me completely miserable with what we had. Are you going to say what I think you are?"

He grinned. "It's Christ. We must have Him as a partner in our marriage or we'll fail again. It's too deep a relationship to be workable without the most important part. But are you willing? I don't think—"

She pushed away from his arms. "Irish, I am going to be a Christian. Right now I'm still getting it all together, and I can't make any promises until I understand what I'm promising, but I can see it's really the only honest way to live."

"Honest?"

"Yes, and I guess there's still more I need to say to you to be completely honest. Last night," her voice trailed away and she gulped. "On the mountain, when you said you'd take my guilt, you had the most terrible expression on your face. At that moment guilt ceased being a bad feeling that disturbed me continually, and it became a real and tangible thing in my life that I have to do something about. But over the burden of it, all night long, I kept seeing your face." She looked up at him and leaning forward she touched one finger to his lips. "Do you know your lips are different?"

He pressed her fingers against his lips and then asked, "How?"

"There's a tenderness about them." She studied his face again and slowly said, "They're no longer tight and hard, but there is a relaxed softness. They look as if they've been hurt to the place where there can be no greater hurt."

She shoved at the tears trickling out of the corners of her eyes. Quickly she continued. "I started to explain. Ever since you've been here, you've been pushing your ideas of God on me. I was completely turned off. It was just the same overbearing male pushing his ideas down my throat. But last night, on the mountain, all those things about God and Christ became alive. It took a lot of thinking about it, and it took Gramps to put into words all that I was seeing. He said that I was seeing the atonement illustrated. He made me see that the horror in your face over the guilt was a small reflection of how Jesus Christ must feel when He takes our sin. It became real. The atonement was not just words, but it became a significant action that really took place.

"You see, until then I thought my guilt was too big for God to forgive. But you forgave me and were even willing to accept responsibility for it all, and you are just another human like me. Irish, I know what hate is." She rubbed at her face and said, "When it sunk in that you were forgiving Karen, the murderer, not Karen, the nice girl, then I knew I could believe God really holds forgiveness for me too."

He watched her silently, his eyes searching out the truth of everything she was saying. She allowed the probing, knowing there was no longer any need to hide. The lines on his forehead eased, but she saw the final question coming. "Meditation?"

Strangely apart, she looked at him, accepting the separation that one word caused. Never would he be able to comprehend all that she had experienced.

"It's gone, forever. How can I explain it?" Her voice dropped to a whisper. "Since I've been able to take one objective, mental step away from it all, I've realized it is a psychological trap.

"You see, at first I thought that Being is God, but I began to have doubts." She paused and looked out over the rocks and trees, feeling as if for one last time she was trying to see beyond it all. "I've had this experience. Every once in a while," she said slowly, "I've been aware of something or someone surrounding me. It was really just a sensation of not being alone, but it was real enough that I've caught myself looking for that someone. And it has made me think. I started wondering why I didn't experience that feeling while I was meditating. Jonathan first made me realize God wouldn't be in meditation."

Irish frowned, "I don't follow you."

"Jonathan first told me the Bible teaches Jesus is God and that the only way to God is through Him. Meditation teaches that He was only a great teacher. I guess I realized back then that meditation was wrong, but I just wasn't willing to surrender that illusion of peace when the alternative I knew was fear.

"I still don't understand all the workings of meditation, but I know ultimately it's a failure. I guess I sensed that almost from the beginning, but they wouldn't let me accept it. Always there was something more that I must do to make it viable. But it couldn't handle the guilt that continued to hound me. Guilt is not something you can ignore. Life is not something you escape but, instead, something you face and live to the fullest." She could see he was satisfied, and she could quit forever trying to explain the unexplainable.

She even managed a chuckle as she reminisced, "What a frustrating experience! The more I listened to Gramps and Homer, the more I felt as if my views of life through meditation were crumbling just like mud bricks in the rain. Have you tried to salvage substance out of running mud?"

Suddenly she turned and pushed Irish back on the rock. "Hey," he protested weakly. She followed him down, her lips seeking his and clinging. When she finally moved and sat up he asked, "Why?"

"Can't you understand? Didn't you sense how fearful I was of your touch?" He nodded and she studied his face. She was guessing his hidden anxiety and the relief of having it all said. "Irish, my love was buried in hate, but more than that, that horrible circumstance paralyzed every emotion into fear. Being close to you brought the horror out where I had to face it. It won't be that way anymore. There, is that faith? Do you believe that?"

He reached for her and she came willingly. When he finally released her, she knew he was convinced.

He got slowly to his feet, pulling her with him. "Karen, do you remember when you first came back to Denver you used a strange word. It's been nagging at me since then. You said you came back to be a servant, only a servant. While I was doing all that reading in the Bible, I found a counterpart to it. Jesus told His disciples—when they finally got to the place that they really believed He was the promised Messiah—He would call them servants no longer, but instead friends.

"That's what Jesus Christ wants of us now. Honest friends, you and me and Jesus Christ." He grinned down at her and taking her hand he said, "Jesus Christ, I'd like You to meet my wife. This is Karen."